# TASTING GRETEL

## LIDIYA FOXGLOVE

# Chapter One

GRETEL

I LOVED GOING TO CHURCH, but not for the reasons I should. In fact, I believe that somewhere in the holy writ it said women should be humble. But no one paid any attention to that.

Every girl in our small town of Aupenburg had one fine outfit for Sundays, the blouse edged with homemade lace, the apron perfectly clean, and the richly dyed wool dress adorned with embroidery. For an unmarried girl, it was an advertisement for her skill.

Mine was the best. I don't mean to be arrogant, but it was simply true. I could never just stick to the simple flowers, the time-tested patterns that girls copied from their mothers and grandmothers. Why not be different?

As I walked in, Kurt cast his green eyes my way, and I offered him a secretive smile. He was the tallest man in the room, the brute strength of his farmer's muscles tempered by dark curls and a sensitively curved mouth.

Sadly, when I talked to him it was all "the pigs" this and "the hay" that and nothing else but I certainly dreamed of what we might do in said hay if this wasn't such a very small town with so many wagging tongues.

"C'mon, sit down," Hansel said, giving me a good-natured little shove. "I'm pretty sure you're not supposed to make your eyes look like that in church."

He was teasing me, but he meant what he said. He didn't like me smiling at boys.

"It's just Kurt. I do absolutely *nothing* and you act like I'm on the brink of becoming the town hussy."

"It's the way you look at everyone," he said, waving for me to keep my voice down although I was nearly whispering. "It's not modest enough. I just don't want any man thinking he can lay a hand on you."

"Well, maybe I wouldn't mind Kurt's hand on me."

"You shouldn't think about things like that until you're married."

I snorted. "What a wedding night it would be if I had never thought about it once until that day."

He frowned. "Let's talk about this when we're not at church."

"Very well."

We were the same age, Hansel and I. Twins, although we didn't look alike. I had as much right to boss him around as he had to boss me, but somehow he always got the final say in my behavior as well as his own. And Hansel was hardly a saint himself, but I didn't realize the extent of it yet.

I settled in the old family pew to bask in a precious morning of beauty. All the women were as colorful as birds. The congregation sung soaring, melancholy hymns. The ceiling was painted with scenes of St. Yktrin, who had grown up in the region. She blessed the whores (who were depicted half naked with pert nipples, an odd subject to ponder during the service), cut the head off a small dragon, and died when she was torn into four pieces by an especially wicked faery king, before ascending to the clouds in a big fancy gold crown. It was quite sensational viewing. Every time I looked at those pictures, I wished I could afford paint.

No, we were poor, but when my mother died, I inherited her box of threads. They must have been one of her wedding gifts, because she had so many colors. I knew it could not have been an everyday sort of purchase. But as long as I could remember, she had thread, and she embroidered dresses and pillows and the edges of my father's Sunday suits.

I continued the tradition. I had been embroidering dresses since I was a little girl, growing out of them only to improve on the next one. At nineteen years of age, I had a masterwork of a dress. It was a simple dark green but the skirt was embroidered with an entire scene: a tree spread across the back of my skirt, with all of our native songbirds perched in the branches, and a pattern of little white edelweiss and red wild roses dancing along the whole hem. The flowers were repeated on the bodice, with two falcons in flight on my shoulders.

I remember how Hansel grinned when he saw them. "Falcons, Gretel? What message does that send? Songbirds would be a better subject than birds of prey."

"I just like them. And they're beautiful."

I was a quiet girl, and if I really had the spirit of a bird of prey, I suppose we wouldn't be so hungry.

For we were hungry, increasingly so. Mother died when we were eight, and our father died when we were fourteen. Although Hansel was a tall, robust boy, he was not prepared to manage the farm. He was good at many things: telling tales, dancing the night away, managing our money, throwing a good punch. The subtleties of nature, on the other hand, eluded him. That first year, he didn't harvest the wheat soon enough, and we lost most of the crop. He was better at hunting, and that was how we survived.

I tried to take on the vegetable garden, but I was hopeless. I had never been very strong. Maybe it was hard to strengthen up when we never had enough to eat. The heat made me dizzy. My mind wandered as I weeded. Neighbors stopped by and I talked to them for too long, drinking cups of tea or small beer in the shade.

That winter, we might have starved, if not for the kindness of those neighbors, and how much Hansel and I loved each other. When I was discouraged, he picked me up, and I did the same for him. One of us was always strong enough to go on, and drag the other forward.

The next year was a little better, but we still had to sell some valuables to buy enough wheat for the winter. We talked of selling the farm and doing something else with our lives, but this was our childhood home, and we weren't sure what else could be done. Learning a new trade and forging a new path was no easy task, and we would have almost certainly been separated.

Every year, we improved, but we always owed someone money, and we had to carefully juggle our debts so that no one was left wanting for long. Hansel was brilliant at this, and he did everything he could to prove himself to the townsfolk that he was trying. We worked so hard. So very hard, all the time, and our bellies never stopped growling. I struggled with the hoe and the weeds by day and took in piecework at night after I had cooked our dinner. We were peasants, no better or worse off than most, in the end. But on Sundays, I looked at the falcons on my shoulders and thought, *I want a big nest at the top of the tree, not a little one in the shrubs.*

There were things I wanted so badly, and I hardly had names for them. They came to me when I created things, and they came to me when I passed by Kurt working in his family fields with his shirt stripped off and his trousers tight. For some reason, it was a similar feeling in both instances. I didn't understand why. It was like I wanted to climb into the colors of the thread and I wanted to climb into Kurt's trousers, but then...neither was quite right.

After the service on that Sunday afternoon, I brushed Hansel off and chatted with friends and admired the summer flowers pinned in everyone's hair. Much to my delight, Lucia invited me and some other girls to a picnic. I would get a good meal out of it, and time to relax.

As I was walking home, taking the long way around the house to look for wild blackberries, I heard a grunting noise behind the stables. We hadn't owned a horse in years, so this was curious.

I peered around the corner.

Hansel was back there thrusting his cock into Peter Bauer's ass.

Yes, my dear brother, who had just seen fit to give me a lecture because my eyes dared to briefly considered the physical beauty of Kurt Fischer, was screwing his best friend like a wolf in heat.

A feeling of overwhelming fury and despair shot through me, and I ripped off my apron and threw it at them. I had forgotten the pockets were full of blackberries. They scattered everywhere. Hansel and Peter scrambled apart, poor Peter flushed to his ears.

"Don't tell my father!" Peter begged me. "Or my mother! Oh, God."

"I won't tell *anyone*. Don't you worry about *that*."

"Gretel—" Hansel was fumbling with the buttons on his trousers. "What are you doing here?"

"What am *I* doing here? This is our property! I'm home from the picnic. And I see you've been keeping busy!"

"It's not— Let me explain."

"Go home, Peter," I said, more gently. "I promise. I won't tell anyone." Peter was a nice boy. I didn't want to ruin his afternoon.

Hansel and I walked into the house in sullen silence, our shoes thudding on dirt floors covered with layers of rushes. It was a beautiful, sunny afternoon with a thousand and two things to be done in the gardens and fields, and we would be sorry later that they weren't being done now.

I crossed my arms. "I don't—"

"It's true," he said. "I thought you sort of knew."

"What, that you're—"

"I've always been—different—you know—bad with girls."

We both sort of faltered. I didn't really know any words for men who liked other men, except a few I didn't want to use on my own brother.

"I don't care," I said. "That's your business."

"Then why did you throw your apron at me?"

"Because you're so protective and critical of me! You notice every little movement of my eyes. Knowing this, I should think, you of all people would not expect me to be a good little maiden every second. I want—I want—to be touched." I stammered. I wanted more than that. I wanted things I couldn't explain. "I wanted to go to the spring festival in Hausach. Maybe I'd find a good husband if I could get out of the village."

There was a little soup left from last night. He doled

some into a bowl. "If you don't have someone to chaperone you and introduce you, you'll only get into trouble."

"You think I can't handle myself? I'm not stupid. I'll carry a knife."

He snorted. "A knife? You think that's going to stop anyone?" He took a big spoonful of the soup. He was starving, as I would have been without the picnic. Hell, I was still starving. I could have eaten every dish at that picnic.

I thought about Peter's flushed skin.

"You don't want to stop anyone, do you?" Hansel snapped. He slunk into a chair and stirred the thin broth. "You look at Kurt like you'd let him do anything to you."

"How long have you and Peter been doing this kind of thing?"

He flung himself out of his chair, his face red. "If you say anything about Peter again, I'll—"

"You'll what? Hit me? I wasn't insulting Peter. I was just asking you a question."

Hansel would never hurt me. But he did something worse. He dashed his bowl of soup to the ground.

Making the food stretch and turning it into something was my job, so when he ruined his meal, it was as good as a slap in the face. My jaw trembled.

"It's—it's your problem if you want to go to bed hungry," I managed.

"Why don't you marry Kurt?" he snapped. "He has more food than we do."

"As if you want me to marry Kurt."

"I'm fine with you marrying him. Just let *him* court *you*."

"I don't even like him. He's stupid. Well, not stupid, but he's like everyone else in this town. He doesn't think about anything beyond what he's always been told and always known. We wouldn't have anything to talk about."

"You're never going to get married, then," Hansel said. "You want someone who is rich, *and* handsome, *and* appreciates your handiwork, *and* indulges you in long conversations about things beyond what you know. Heavens, if such a man exists, I'll fight you for him. You're just going to be an old maid. At least you *can* marry," he said. "Any man you like."

"And you can fuck any man you like. I can't indulge my urges without risking pregnancy and being thought of as the town whore. I don't think you understand what it's like to have—feelings—you don't understand, and can't act on."

"You think I don't understand that?" he snapped. "I have it worse than you, I think."

"But you're a boy! Girls must be so good and obey the men, all the time. You want me to obey you; you won't let me go anywhere on my own."

His mouth crumpled briefly before he mastered himself again. "I don't want you to obey me. I just *need* you to—stop messing around with dreams that will never come true. I *do* know how it is to have feelings you don't understand. I know more about that than you'll *ever* know."

"I'm not so sure," I said bitterly. "And believe me, I wish you could marry Peter. His family grows a lot more wheat than we do. Maybe if you had a husband he could salvage this mess we've gotten ourselves into."

Hansel sat down, kicked the soup bowl all the way across the room, and started to cry.

Pain shot through me at the sound. I hadn't heard Hansel cry in years, I realized. He had always had a tender heart and he used to cry all the time when he was younger, but he had just stopped doing it, and I never noticed until this sudden reappearance.

*It was when he got close with Peter,* I realized. *He takes all his cares and troubles to Peter instead of worrying me.*

I took a cautious step toward him, but I wasn't sure what to say.

We both wanted things we couldn't have. We had been born to a farm and neither of us were suited to it. Where did we go from here?

I lapsed back into silence. I was comfortable in silence. Whenever we tried to talk out our problems, they only grew worse. I picked up the bowl Hansel had overturned and wiped the soup off the side with my napkin, then returned it to him. There was still some soup in the bottom he might want to scrape up.

When he stopped crying, I said gently, "I just want to find some way we can be happy. This way isn't working. I know neither of us want to give up this little house. All our memories are here. But—"

"Peter is leaving town." He interrupted me with those four words, and he spoke them like he was drowning under them.

"Why?"

"He says there are no opportunities here. He wants to go to Hausach and find work."

"He's smart," I said.

"Well, maybe so." He put his head in his hand and stared at the empty bowl. "I'm sorry. I shouldn't have done that."

"I'm sorry, too. I didn't know. I—I shouldn't have said those things. You love him, don't you?"

"Yes..." He stood up decisively, walked over to me, and put a heavy hand on my head. "In a different way than I love you, of course, but no more. I just don't want to leave you to the fate of so many girls who are poor and have few options. If I went to Hausach...you won't be able to reach me if you're in trouble."

Sometimes I couldn't believe the extent of his protectiveness. He thought I would stay here alone? I knew what he was thinking; that if I went to the city, I'd get into trouble. "Hansel, if you go to Hausach, for heaven's sake, I'm leaving too. You want to follow him?" I asked.

He nodded.

"Maybe this is for the best. We have to do something, unless we want to grow old and very, very skinny together here on this sad excuse for a farm. I'm good with my fingers. I can find a respectable apprenticeship working with thread if given half a chance, I'm sure."

He huffed. "I know you're right. But this is all we have, this is all our family has ever had..."

"I know, but...it's not working. I wish I wasn't right, but you know I am."

"All right. We'll sell the farm."

I kissed his cheek.

"You look sad now," he said.

"I'm happy...," I said, taking in the small room where I had learned to sew and cook. Where my parents had laid in state before burial. Where I had sobbed into the pillow and stared out the window imagining a better life. "But sometimes it does feel surprisingly similar."

# Chapter Two

GRETEL

AFTER WE SOLD the farm and paid our debts, there was not much left. All that we owned now fit in two sacks. We set out with hard bread and hard cheese, and enough coin for more of the same. Neither of us had ever left the village, but now we had a long journey ahead to the port city of Hausach. Aupenburg was surrounded by the forests that stretched across three kingdoms. It had many names: the Secret Forest, the Green Death, and here, the Shadow-Wald.

Hansel had bought us a map, and he kept talking about the map like it was an assurance of safety. The moment I started to wonder if the bears would smell our food, or whether we could walk fast enough to reach shelter for the night, he would say, "It'll be all right. We have the map. We'll stick to the Queen's Road."

Friends and neighbors waved us goodbye. Kurt asked me to write him, but I knew he was barely capable of writing back. We set off down the path to meet the Royal Road, and Aupenburg disappeared behind the pines.

We trudged along, exchanging comments on unusual roadside mushrooms or cheerfully noting the presence of familiar farmsteads, for at this point we were not far from home.

Then, the forest seemed to grow thicker and darker and older. The trees blotted out the sun almost entirely. The air grew cooler and smelled of moist leaves and ancient, unfamiliar life. Vines crawled into the path; leaves and pinecones littered the old pave-stones and then the stones ended altogether.

Hansel looked at the map. "It looks as if we keep going straight to reach the Queen's Road."

"Are you sure we didn't miss the fork?"

"Did you see anything that looked like a fork?"

"No."

"Well, Gretel, what else do you want me to say?"

"I—just—I don't know. This barely looks like a road at all. I'm wondering if we were supposed to turn somewhere and we missed it. Maybe the sign fell."

"So you're saying we should turn back? But the last homestead must have been two hours behind us."

"Shouldn't we have reached Pillna by now?"

By the way, following a map is a great way to bond with a loved one. I highly recommend it if you want it all to end in a suicide pact. We must have spent twenty minutes arguing over the map as the sun crept lower and lower. Soon we were squinting at the parchment in the waning light.

Finally, we decided it was better to turn back and find the last homestead before the sun went down. At worst, we would lose a few hours and would have to sleep in their barn. That sounded better than getting eaten by wolves.

But as we were walking, we thought we noticed something that might have been the fork in the road to reach Pillna. There was no sign. No wonder we missed it; we had been looking for a *road*, not a path. An old pile of horse droppings indicated that it must go somewhere.

We decided to make an attempt to reach Pillna before the sun went down.

I had never walked so much in one day. I was sweating, stray hairs flying out of my golden braids.

Hansel kept looking at me.

"What?" I said.

"Nothing."

"Nothing? Why do you keep looking at me like that?"

His legs, longer and stronger than mine, forged up a steep section of rocky pathway. Then he turned and offered his hand to me. "I'm thinking how I might have made a terrible mistake. How we might die in this damn forest."

"We're not—going—to die," I panted, gripping his arm.

"It's almost dark. I shouldn't have brought you along."

"So you can die alone?"

"I might have made it, on my own. If I didn't, at least—"

"You think we're going to die because I slowed us down?" I put my hands on my knees, catching my breath. "If we die out here, it's because we have a stupid map for these stupid roads."

"It's not your fault you're fragile," he said.

"I'm not fragile."

"I just don't want you to get hurt because of *me*," he said. "I should have insisted that you stay at home where it's safe, where you belong. You should have married Kurt. Why can't you just be satisfied with that?"

I made a sharp exhalation of anger. "This is my choice," I said. "How many times do I have to tell you, I don't want to live and die in *Aupenburg!*"

We walked in silence. Darkness fell fast in the forest, because it was already so dark to begin with, and deep down I wondered if he was right. I didn't want to die in Aupenburg, but I definitely didn't want to die in the middle of the forest.

"A light," he whispered.

"What?" I wasn't sure I'd heard him right.

"Look, in the distance."

Now I saw it too. Two lights, actually. Candles burning in the deepening dusk.

We picked up our pace. By the time we reached the source of the light, it was almost entirely dark, but the candles were in mirrored lanterns that amplified their glow. They illuminated the door of the most beautiful cottage I had ever seen.

The entire cottage was painted, first white so it stood out in the dark forest, and then with little scenes. Dancing maidens, musicians, ships pulling into harbor, foxes and bears and deer peering out of trees: those were the door panels, clearly lit by the candles. The rest was painted too, with patterns of flora and fauna in knot-like designs.

"Faery art, isn't it?" Hansel said warily. "What is this doing out here?" Faeries were more prevalent to the north and west.

But perhaps even more alluring than the art was something neither of us could resist: the aroma of chocolate, so thick and dark and luscious that I wondered if I was dreaming. I imagined this was the smell of the royal patisseries in the grandest cities in the realm, and here it was, in the middle of the forest.

"I don't like this," Hansel said. "This has to be witchcraft."

"I'd rather die eating enchanted chocolate than be eaten by forest beasts," I said. I knocked on the door.

The door opened for us, but no one was there. Even I got a little nervous at that. But it only lasted a moment. "Look!" I gasped.

The interior was well lit with candles and a counter was spread with chocolates and pastries. It looked like the interior of a shop. No one in the world could have resisted the smell of sugar and butter and toasted nuts that wafted out. The cakes were uncut and sitting out to cool in a row, seven of them, all swathed in icing. The candies were absolutely countless. Truffles and bon bons caked in chopped nuts and coconut, colorful ribbons of crackling sugar, neat squares of caramel. Many of these things I had only seen in a cookbook and not in real life.

It was a feast for every sense I had. Not just the smell and the promise of their taste, but the pure sight of all their colors and textures...

"Don't touch," Hansel growled behind me.

I glared at him. My hands hadn't moved—yet. But he knew me too well.

Then, I heard a distinct male chuckle behind one of the doors to the interior of the house. Hansel and I instinctively edged closer together.

Old hinges creaked open. A faery man walked in.

I wondered how I could have ever found Kurt Horner attractive.

He was tall, with dark curls that were just long enough to run my fingers through, and golden eyes that drove into my heart the moment they sought mine—which was immediately. He was not as strapping as the farm boys back home, but radiated a more complex strength, as if he had magic along with some muscle, and a considerable amount of grace as well. He moved like he knew how to dance. He had enough experience with life that he knew almost everything about a person the moment he laid eyes on them. At least, that was how it felt.

His clothes were the only disappointment. Faeries were known for their elegant and beautiful clothing, but he wore nothing but a sturdy gray shirt and black trousers with a flour-dusted apron over them. He might have been our town baker, in that regard.

"Good evening," he said. "Lost, are we?" He turned to Hansel now, after looking at me long enough to weaken my knees. "Maps only go so far when the roads are always changing."

"My name is Hansel and this is my sister. We're looking for Pillna," Hansel said.

"Pillna," the man said. "Yes. I can point you there in the morning."

"If you have a place for us to sleep and maybe a bite to eat, well, we can't offer much, but—"

"I don't need your coin. You're welcome to my table."

"Thank you, sir," Hansel said. His words were a little sharp. He was still suspicious. Any sensible person would have been. For some reason, I was not.

The man opened the door and held it for us. Hansel went ahead. When I passed through, the baker gave me another look. One that I knew was not meant for Hansel to see. He assessed me with his eyes, and it made me shudder to my toes.

*He's weighing me,* I thought. *Do I measure up?* I didn't know what he wanted. But whatever it was, I hoped I was worthy. Everything about this place was a dream to me. It was surprising and beautiful at every turn.

There was something dark about the faery man

himself, and that should have made me hesitate. I should not have wanted to run toward that shadow. His eyes were full of strange knowledge, and I wanted to know it too. *I would never be a mere farm girl if I knew what he knew*, I thought.

I felt as if he was that elusive thing I had been looking for all my life. I still didn't quite know what it meant. The feeling rumbled through me like far off thunder preceding a much-needed rain.

He was very polite as he showed us to the table. It was already set with a generous spread, as if we were expected. We took the chairs flanking him, to enjoy roast leg of venison and plenty of different vegetables with ample butter and seasonings, things we could never dream of affording.

"It's unusual to have company for dinner," he said.

"Do you usually eat all of this yourself?" Hansel asked.

"No, no. I put whatever is left out for the other wood folk," he said.

"I didn't know faeries have to put food out for other faeries," I said, amused.

"There are different sorts of faeries," he said. "Civilized faeries like myself share food with the wood faeries."

"Who are all the cakes for?" Hansel asked.

"It is a bargain I have made," he said. "If I spend my days making cakes, I can live here."

"A bargain? What sort of bargain?"

"Are you a dinner guest or an interrogator?" the faery man asked. "You should learn to relax, Hansel." He filled Hansel's glass with wine. Then he looked at me again. "You never told me your name."

"Gretel."

"Gretel. It seems a very workaday name for you."

"I am workaday, I'm afraid."

"Are you?"

"What's—your name, sir?" I stammered, trying to shake off the renewed sense that he could read my mind.

"Who says I have one?" he said, with a tinge of regret. "Names are lost to men who are mere shadows. I am just the baker of the Shadow-Wald and that is all. Call me simply 'the Magus'."

The Magus did not sound simple at all, not the way he said it. It was a seductive and confident purr of a word, and I had to restrain myself from testing it right then and there. *The Magus...*

"You're a mage too?" I asked.

"Yes," he said.

"What kind of magic do you do?"

"A very specialized kind."

Hansel's fork clinked noisily against his plate and I quickly looked down to cut up my venison. Hansel didn't like me talking to this man. He suspected something was afoot, and perhaps he was right. Nothing about this place made sense; a faery man making cakes worthy of a palace out in a tiny cottage in the woods?

The way the Magus looked at me made my pulse race and my body ache with desire. I wished I was wearing my embroidered gown so I looked my best, but it was still in my pack for safekeeping. I felt in some odd way as if I already knew him, and he already knew me. All the little fantasies I'd had about Kurt now seemed like practice for a man like this, and somehow I knew that if we were alone, he would indulge them. Could I get Hansel out of the way?

I jammed a chunk of potato with my fork. *Of course not. He's watching your every move, as he always does. And besides, this is ridiculous. You don't know this man. You can't risk pregnancy with a stranger before you go to find a respectable job in the city.*

"You are lucky," the Magus said. "You found this place. The forest must have wanted you to come."

"If the forest has a mind of its own, I'll just be glad to leave it," Hansel said.

I saved a little room in the hopes that the Magus would offer us one of his cakes or at least a taste of a bon bon, but when we were done with our food and the warm laziness of the wine had just started going to my head, he said, "Well, I should make up your beds."

"Thank you again for your generosity," Hansel said, in a formal tone. Despite his suspicions, of course he didn't want to be impolite to a faery mage.

The Magus left the table and I heard his footsteps creak up the stairs. Even that humble sound was alluring when I knew the footsteps belonged to such long, graceful legs.

"You are as pink as a rose," Hansel said. "Whatever you're thinking, try to stop thinking it."

"As long as I can control my actions, I see no need to control my thoughts," I said.

"I wonder what he meant by that names business," Hansel said. "What did he say? Men with shadows don't have names...I can't remember, but it sounded like riddles. What, he doesn't have any name at all?"

"Names are especially important to the fair folk," I said. "They use them for spells. I'm sure it's some custom we don't know much about."

"It has something to do with whoever lets him stay here in exchange for baking cakes, I suppose," Hansel said. "I sure don't like this place. We're leaving at first light."

"Of course..." I thought of the tales about eating faery food and being trapped in their realm forever. But those were old stories. Faeries were more civilized these days.

Was it terrible that I wished they were true?

The Magus returned momentarily as a clock chimed somewhere in the house. "Upstairs, the little room on the left, I've made up for you with a bed for each. I hope it suffices and you have a good rest."

"The privy is out back?" Hansel asked, with a wary glance at me.

"Yes," the Magus said. "Out the back door in the hall, there."

"I'll meet you in the bedroom, Gretel," Hansel said pointedly.

Well, I knew I'd only have a minute or two with the Magus, but I was eager for them.

But the Magus left the room even before Hansel did. When the back door shut, I took a few brisk steps to catch up with him just before he vanished through another door. He jerked back when he heard me coming. I touched his arm. His skin was cold. "Magus, I just wanted to ask—"

"*Don't* touch me."

It was too late. Where my fingers had brushed his forearm, a line of angry welts appeared, like I burned him.

"I don't understand," I said.

He made no move to explain, but quietly rolled his sleeve down and buttoned the cuff. "Do you need something, Gretel?"

"Where do you make all the cakes?"

"Here." He swung the door open to a kitchen. The oven had a large door to put the cakes in but also a smooth surface on top for pots. The fire must be built in the bottom portion and vented out through a pipe. The long table was dusted with flour and littered with bowls and canisters and jars holding nuts and spices and candied flower petals. The room was stuffy with heat but it smelled marvelous and was such a nice airy space, the walls painted white with cheerful scenes of a feast, that I wished I could stay and watch him work.

"You are still hungry, aren't you?" the Magus said. "You saved space for dessert."

"Oh, that was more food than I've had in ages already," I said, trying to be polite.

I already knew there was no fooling him, however. Our mouths said words while our eyes had the true conversation.

He lifted a glass case and picked up a truffle with a pair of small tongs. He lifted the truffle to my mouth. I opened wide. The chocolate smelled dark and almost smoky as it drew near my nose. The truffle started melting in my mouth the moment it touched my tongue. I closed my lips and broke the delicate underside of it with the tip of my tongue and was met with dark chocolate and syrup-coated cherries. It was not as sweet as I expected. Bitter and sour, as much as sweet, and yet quite possibly the most delicious thing I'd ever tasted.

"Your brother will be coming back in any minute and I'd rather not get into a brawl with him," the Magus said. "You should go to bed."

I nodded, my mouth too full to speak, and went to the bedroom. Two beds, nicer than the ones we had left behind, stood on either side of a window. The truffle melted away in no time, but the taste lingered. Hansel tromped up the stairs noisily but by that time I had already taken off my outer layer and slipped under the covers in my shift, my head on the pillow. Innocent as I could manage.

"It is a nice room, at least," Hansel said as he took off his shoes, regarding the beeswax candles burning on the nightstand, their fragrance much sweeter than the tallow we could barely afford. Generous piles of blankets topped the bed, so we could choose what thickness we wanted. It was summer now, but in the forest the night was still very cool.

"Everything here is very nice and cozy," I said, and it was. But "nice" and "cozy" also seemed ridiculous words for this atmosphere. It was like saying the Shadow-Wald was green and pretty.

"I'll blow out the candles, then?"

"Yes, goodnight."

He knocked out both flames with one puff and climbed under the covers.

I tried to shut my eyes. The moon shone directly between a crack in the curtains. I was restless, my body ready for something. My nipples were hard and—ahh—I stroked my wet sex, imagining faery hands caressing me. Hansel was soon breathing deeply in sleep, while I rubbed my clit, sliding deeper into my desires. My tongue still tasted bitter.

I heard wheels sliding on uneven road and hoof-beats outside. The door opened downstairs. Then I heard the Magus say, "We must be quiet. I have guests tonight."

"Guests?" a man replied.

"A human brother and sister. Lost on their way to Pillna."

"Brother and sister, eh? A lost girl who found her way to your door? What's she like?" A pause. "A truffle is missing." Then, "You fed her a truffle."

"She has somewhere to be. I would not entrap her here."

"But that is exactly what you're meant to do. My lord, please don't lose heart. Not after all I've done to bring you back. You look so pale."

"Time is running out for me."

"You will feel better the moment you taste her sweet sex."

I stroked myself harder at the thought of his mouth there. Hansel would be so horrified, but Hansel was one to talk. Hansel expected me to be chaste and good, when he was anything but. Hansel was going to be with Peter.

"It will only be torture," the Magus said. "For both of us."

"My lord, I know your current position chafes, but if you found yourself the right maiden you would be so strong again that the Wicked Revels would belong to you as much as anyone. I had all of this planned out! You need to use your magic. If you became valuable to the people, your position would be strong and we could make our move."

The Magus said in a commanding tone, "Take your cakes and go on. I have work to do."

"Of course, my lord, of course," the man said, with faint chagrin. I heard floor boards and doors creak as the desserts were walked in and out. When he was gone, I tried to finish, but my mind was now wandering too much into other questions.

I had heard of the Wicked Revels. A hidden realm where the fair folk danced the night away and made love with abandon. Sometimes the gates opened for humans. In the Wicked Revels, inhibitions were shed. Proper behavior, proper attire, proper manners: all these things meant nothing to the revelers. The rumor was that occasionally, a girl would go there and never return, because she married a faery and spent the rest of her life dancing and feasting in the land of endless joy. Supposedly that was how the kingdom of Torina lost their youngest princess.

It sounded like the Magus needed me. Needed to taste me. Needed "the right maiden". But my touch burned him.

I wasn't quite sure what all of this entailed, but I ached to find out.

Magus didn't go to bed that night. Down in the kitchen, I heard the occasional whacking of a knife or the metal clank of oven doors or tools for tending the fire. The clock chimed the hour. I seemed to drift in and out of sleep throughout the night, and at four in the morning I decided to pad downstairs.

The Magus was pouring a pot of melted chocolate into a broad pan with a short brim. The warm chocolate seeped into the corners of the pan and he smoothed it with a spatula. Then he looked up and wiped his hands on his apron as he strolled around to the front of the table and leaned against it. "Gretel," he said.

"Magus, I—I couldn't sleep." I was working up to asking him the question.

"Nor could I."

"I couldn't help but overhear..." I rubbed my arms. "You said that we wouldn't have found our way here if the forest didn't want us to..."

"You want to stay," he said, cutting out all the preamble.

"Yes. I do."

"You don't know what you're agreeing to."

"Then tell me."

"What I need from you will be torturous," he said.

Heat stoked inside me. "What do you mean?"

"I need your desire," he said. "I need you to feel it burning within you like a star. If I had the magic of your desire, my confections would be an irresistible aphrodisiac for the dancers of the Wicked Revels, but my magic is sapped because I have nothing to feed it. But you see, your desire will only be stoked. Never fed. I can't touch you.

Not even through a glove. And I am forbidden from bringing you complete satisfaction."

"Forbidden? Who forbids you from touching me?"

"The King of the Revels."

"Why?"

"To make a long story into a short one, I once tried to seduce his wife, before they were ever married. I will tell you the long story later, over a glass of wine, if you choose to stay."

"So we—we just look at each other and feel desire and never touch?"

"More than that," he said. "I have many ways of stoking your desire and I will make use of them. I will test how close to the brink I can drive you. Again, and again... and again." He walked closer. "I am very good at this."

"What will you do?"

"If I tell you, half the fun of it is lost. But I think you can imagine some things I might do. If you don't think this will bring you pleasure, if it doesn't intrigue you far more than it concerns you, then you are not the right girl for the task."

*I am very good at this.* I'll bet he was. I was turned on just looking at him, at his simplest gestures—the finger tapping on the counter, the legs crossing as he leaned. I wanted to know why my touch burned him. I wanted to see if he could, indeed, drive me to the brink. It was a challenge. I was not easily driven anywhere.

But if anyone could, he was the one.

"It does intrigue me," I said, my voice a low whisper.

"Does it," he said, not so much a question as two careful words, poking at my resolve. "You are very hungry, and I have plenty to eat. If you are intrigued for the wrong reasons, you will regret it deeply. Tell me and I will give you an ample supply of food and send you on your way."

"I am *not* agreeing for the wrong reasons," I said. "It's easy enough to find bread. Some other things I wish for are harder to find."

"Do you realize what I'm asking of you?"

"You are offering me endless anticipation without satisfaction."

"Yes, Gretel. Why do you want such a life?"

"Because..." I struggled to explain. "I have wanted to be an artist. We could barely afford paint, so I embroidered dresses instead. It was the only medium I had. So I plan out the pattern, and I get to work, and I see it all take shape...and then it's done. It never looks as beautiful as I thought it would, and worse...it's over. It's just over and there is nothing more to produce. I hate that part. Food is much the same. The best part of a meal is the moment you sit down and look at it and smell it and know you're about to eat it. Anticipation is the best part of life. "

"But what if you never got to eat it?" He narrowed his eyes at me. "That is my situation and I wouldn't wish it on anyone. I am forbidden from having anything I really want."

"I want to stay, Magus. Please. Is there some special word I have to speak?"

This was the first time he looked like he believed I might actually stay, and it was marvelous to behold, even though it was just a little light that flared in his eyes. He finally peeled off from the table and walked close to me, looking down at me. It would have felt right if he touched my cheek, but of course he couldn't.

"You swear it, Gretel? You consent to enter this bargain of mutual temptation?"

I didn't hesitate. It was as if I had always known this was a choice, and it was always the choice I would make. This man was full of mysteries, and this place was full of delights, and the life he offered was, as he put it, a torture. I didn't know what he would do to me. I don't know why I wanted this, but I wanted it more than anything. My endless desire to create beauty was already a torture, and somehow I knew he would drive me close to the stars.

"Yes. I swear it."

He gave me a small bow. "So it is."

I wondered what to tell Hansel. He would never understand.

"Go with your brother to Pillna," the Magus said. "Stay at the inn there at the square. Tell the innkeeper, Anna, that you are pledged to me. She will offer you a good job at the inn. It's a pleasant place. Hansel will like it. He will think he's leaving you somewhere that is, in his mind, safe. Bid him goodbye, and then come back to me."

"You have it all worked out," I said.

"I've been waiting for you for three long years," he said. "I didn't think you would come. I certainly didn't think you would be a half-starved slip of a peasant girl. But I shall put some meat on your bones now. Now, you should go back to your bed and get what sleep you can. It's still a long walk to Pillna."

# Chapter Three

GRETEL

OF COURSE, Hansel was up the very moment the sun's light started turning back the darkness. Clearly, he had not heard me go to visit the Magus, but I could tell he still sensed that something was afoot. He hustled me out the door and would not even sit down to breakfast.

As soon as we left, Hansel said, "The way you looked at him, Gretel."

"So, I'm not allowed to think and I'm not allowed to look."

"Don't make it out like I'm the unreasonable one. If you find work at a shop and some handsome man walks in, are you going to draw the proper boundaries?"

"I'm not a silly flirt. Flirting is full of pretense, and I'm terrible at pretense. That's the trouble. I look at people honestly and I try to find the honesty in them. I can't help it. I don't want to have it any other way."

"So, no," he said.

"Are we going to argue about this *again?*"

He frowned. "I'm just glad we're leaving, that's all. That man is dangerous."

I couldn't even feel guilty that I was going against Hansel's wishes for me. I wanted him to be happy with Peter; why couldn't he let me have what I wanted? *Soon it will just be the Magus and me. He will do whatever he must do and I will have to succumb because I've agreed.*

I don't know what sort of strange girl I was, for being so excited by the prospect. But I was no innocent. Besides the things I'd imagined doing with handsome boys, I'd run into my fair share of lecherous men. I could spot danger of that sort. I knew that wasn't what the Magus promised. He promised a dance, elegant and controlled. He promised everything I would never get from a village boy.

We walked all day before reaching Pillna by late afternoon. It was a generously sized town tucked into a valley with the Shadow-Wald looming around it. I guessed it to be double the size of Aupenburg. We spotted the inn from the top of the hill; it was two stories tall with broad exposed beams. Some of the patrons were sitting outside in a courtyard garden. I had never seen that before, eating out of doors. The tiny inn in our town was dim and grubby. By the time we reached the door, I was hopeful that Hansel would go along with my plan. Everything about the inn seemed eminently respectable. Fresh-faced girls set hearty meals and mugs of beer on proper tablecloths, and people of all ages were enjoying the fare in front of three tall windows. Behind the counter, souvenirs of Pillna were on offer: carved forest creatures and plates hand-painted with pictures of the town square.

"We won't be able to afford this place," Hansel said, glancing around with his hands in his pockets, no doubt feeling the weight of our few coins. "We still have a ways to go."

"Maybe we could work for our room," I said.

"They seem to have plenty of workers already."

"Let me try," I said. I asked one of the waitresses for the innkeeper and she brought out a rosy-cheeked, plump woman with auburn hair tucked under a lace cap.

"I'm Anna. What can I do for you?"

Hansel was standing too close. "My brother and I are short on coin," I said. "I wondered if we could work for room and board?"

"We don't—"

I cut her off quickly. "The Magus told us to come to you. Please, madam."

"He did, did he?"

"He gave us directions, that's all," Hansel interrupted. "Do you know the man?"

"Not...well," Anna said. "He's a faery. He keeps to himself. He's a part of the Wicked Revels and some folks would rather they all moved on. But—" She looked at me carefully. "Come on back. Your brother can wash the dishes and you can make the beds."

"Thank you."

Soon I found myself wrestling with large sheets in rooms fit for a nobleman. How did this inn enjoy so much prosperity?

I was fluffing up the pillows when Anna came into the room and shut the door behind me. "Are you the one?" she said.

I straightened. *The one.* A fresh shiver slid down my spine. "The one what?"

"Are you going back to him?"

The pillow slipped from my hands and I turned. "Yes... I want to. He said to tell you—"

She nodded. "I know, dear, I know. You know that means you spent last night in the faery realm? His home is not a part of this world. You found it because you were meant to find it."

"So he said."

"God help you for all of our sakes."

"Why?"

"The doorways to the Wicked Revels have been opening here often. Why should our town play host to the faery realm? It's a curse as much as it's a blessing but don't tell them I said that; certainly my purse has benefited from the Revels. The faeries lure in girls of this town to dance. They slip out even the doors are locked. To keep us from fussing too much about it, the faeries come into town and patronize our business with silver and gold. We're rich because of them. One day *he* came—your Magus. He said he was waiting for someone."

"Do you know why he's waiting for someone?"

"I don't, but he looks to me like a man with something heavy on his shoulders. Some curse, I'd guess. The town will be relieved when the Revels move on, even if it means an end to our fortunes. I can only wish you good luck."

That evening, Hansel could not stop praising the splendid meal and how impressed he was by the cleanliness and organization of the kitchen. He slept well in the tidy little room Anna offered us. When Anna offered me a job in the morning, I could tell he was concerned over my proximity to the Magus, but he couldn't argue with such a respectable establishment.

"This is a good place for you," he said, looking out the windows at the sturdy, well-fed village folk starting their work day as we ate hot porridge and ham. I could tell he was thinking there wasn't much trouble I could get into here, compared to a large port city. I suppose no one had told him about the Revels while he washed dishes.

Despite all of our arguing, I cried when we parted. Hansel and I had been through so much together, and our conflicts were born as much from our tense situation as anything.

"I hope you have a chance to make beautiful things here," Hansel said. "Please write even if the replies are slow to come. I don't know where I'll be."

"The same to you," I said. "I hope you find a way to be with Peter."

"Little sister." He embraced me hard. "Thank you."

"For what?"

"For not judging me for loving him. I know we've argued about...other things. I apologize if my attempts to protect you have only put up a wall between us. But—it means a lot to me that—well, if you think I've sinned, at least you haven't said so."

"Hansel, never!" I said, surprised he would even say that.

"Well, why wouldn't you? I worry over it myself."

"I never pay attention in church, Hans, I'm too busy making eyes," I teased.

I watched him walk away, lingering at the door of the inn.

Then I changed into my Sunday dress and carefully combed my hair until it was a shining river of flaxen gold. I twisted it into a crown of braids and set off down the path from whence I had come.

# Chapter Four

GRETEL

THE COTTAGE DOOR WAS OPEN, framing his tall, lean body. I could see him in the distance. No apron now. He wore all black. He looked completely in control, but radiated a pent excitement.

I fed off him. My body was positively humming by the time I reached the door. My pulse was quick. I was slightly terrified now that the moment was at hand, but every nerve in my body was singing. I knew he was going to make me feel sensations I could never reach on my own. My hand and my imagination were a feeble substitute for the undivided attentions of a man who looked like sex and mystery made flesh. He looked at me like it pained him to tear his eyes away.

"Gretel," he said. "You are my Gretel now."

"Oh..." No one had ever called me such a thing before. It thrilled me to my bones but I wasn't sure if I should betray that yet.

"We are in this together," he said. "I can't satisfy myself the way you could satisfy me, if I we were able to touch."

"Will you...ever be able to touch me?"

"I hope so. But we must enjoy what pleasures we may. Come in. I have carefully planned our afternoon."

*Carefully planned...* I crossed the threshold, and although I had been here before, it all felt very different now.

"You weren't wearing this before," he said, motioning to my dress.

"I wanted to wear my finest for you now."

"You do have skill," he said thoughtfully.

"I hoped I would find some work of this nature in the city," I said. "Until I ended up here instead."

"Quite a change of plans. Not as different a life as one might guess, however. Pleasure is its own sort of art. You're looking for something. I hope you find it here. Follow me." He waved me into the workroom, but now there was a new feature: a wooden rack opposite his work space. It reminded me of a large clock with four hands, two longer and two shorter, each with a restraint at the end. The hands could be moved around, but just now they were all positioned downward in a relaxed position, and it certainly did not escape my notice that they were just the right size and shape to hold my arms and legs.

My desire was already trickling out of me, unbidden. *This is really happening,* I thought. *I will be at his mercy.*

"Take off your clothes," he said.

"All of them?"

"What do you think, my dear? I didn't take you for a girl who would ask questions you already know the answer to."

I flushed, embarrassed.

"You don't need to feign coyness here," he said. "I know you are as excited as I am."

I started unfastening the hooks at my bodice. He watched me for a moment as my hands trembled. The bodice loosened around my ribcage and although I was not some rich and idle girl who wore her clothes too tight just to look pretty, in this moment I was glad not to feel fabric clenching around me. I needed to breathe.

He crossed around to the other side of the table and picked up a bowl of chestnuts, slitting the skins with a sharp knife. His eyes only left me for brief seconds.

I paused. "Don't cut yourself."

His eyes squinted with amusement. "If I do, it's for a good cause."

I pulled the embroidered wool dress over my head, and then the softer, thinner gown beneath. I was down to my linen shift and good petticoat. I reached for my shoes.

"No, no, my Gretel," he said. "The shoes come last."

Somehow, I had already known he wouldn't let me get away with that. I let the petticoat drop to the floor and pulled off the shift, baring myself to him. No man had ever seen me like this before, but I disliked my innocence. I would have shed it long ago if I could. I smothered my hesitations, letting him admire me and resisting the urge to shield myself, even my imperfections. I was certainly too thin, and my face and arms had suffered from many sunburns, leaving me with freckles and something of an agitated tan there, while from breasts to legs I was white as milk. No lady would have tolerated such an appearance.

I am not sure he saw any of that. He looked at me like I was everything he had ever yearned for. "That's better," he said. "I know you're not shy. Enough pretending. Are you a virgin, Gretel?"

My mouth pinched in distaste. "I don't like the word.

But yes. I'm not a fool. If I had a baby out of wedlock, well, I'm sure you know what humans think of that."

"You've done other things, then?" he said, almost casually.

"I don't trust the boys in town not to blabber," I said. "So, no."

"But you touch yourself?"

I was a little flustered at his frankness.

He chuckled, sliding the chestnuts into the oven. "All right, then. You are a little shy. Just a little. Go ahead and get your shoes off."

I bent over and unlaced my well-worn boots. I knew he had a nice view of my ass while I did so. I took off my wool stockings, which were really much too warm for this room.

"You are beautiful," he said gruffly, the tone of a man trying not to show how much something affected him. "I have not seen such a sight in years..."

"I've heard faeries are quite promiscuous," I said, wondering how many girls he'd seen and been with before me.

"Generally, yes. The Wicked Revels, in particular, is a place with no inhibitions and every sort of sensory delight." His expression briefly drifted. "The girls there don't wear much. And they liked to catch my eye, back in those days. But there are also rules and codes of conduct, meant to protect the guests." He put down the knife and picked up a smooth stick, rather like a baton or a wand, instead, using it to point me toward the restraints behind me.

"Step back, Gretel. I think you can figure it out."

I swallowed, a wave of trepidation making me sway a little. I had never given up control like this before.

He nudged my hip with the wand. I backed my ankles

up into the restraints. Footholds were built into the arms of the rack, along with little ridges of support to help hold up my upper arms and thighs. Or *were* they to support me? Maybe they were to keep me from closing my thighs once I was trapped. The smooth pieces of wood hugged my bare skin. As soon as I touched the bonds, he tapped the wand and the wood closed around me with a clunk. He pressed my wrists back with the side of the wand, and tapped those restraints as well.

Heat twisted my core. His cock was a stiff shape in his trousers. I already wanted him to do something to me. Anything.

He stood over me, his face drawing closer than we had been before. He put a hand flat on the wall behind me, the plain gray cotton of his shirt strained against his broad shoulder. His golden eyes were beautiful and a little unearthly. I couldn't look at them for too long.

He slid the tip of the wand between the wet folds of my sex. The thin, hard flick of sensation was over too fast. He sucked my juices off the tip.

A faint smile twitched at the edges of his mouth. "That is powerful magic," he said. "If you are not the one, you are, at least, worth a try."

Now he used the wand to guide the restraints. When he touched the tip of the wand to the wood, it locked on like a magnet. He lifted my arms out to my sides and spread my legs wider until I could feel the air on my inner folds and knew my clit was exposed to him.

"It is better not to have anything in the way," he said. "But this won't cut you. It's magic." He opened a drawer of the kitchen cabinet and took out a small golden knife. He crouched before me and slid the blade carefully along the mounds of my pussy, using the tip of the wand to manipulate my folds so he didn't have to touch me. All of this was a terrible tease. I wanted to grab his hair. I already craved his touch so badly that my untouched skin seemed to ache all over. My fingers grasped and clenched at the open air and I drew tense breaths. I felt my juices trickling down my leg. He scraped the tip of the wand along my inner thigh and took another taste.

"Ah, dear one, and this is only the first evening..." He stood up again and now he was so close that just a shift of his hips would have rubbed his cock against my bare stomach. "This is the first evening of the rest of your life with me. How do you feel?"

"I want to be *touched*," I said, unable to pretend.

"You certainly do," he said. "I will know everything you feel. What do you suppose happens when I take this feeling that radiates off of you and turn it into spell work that goes into every confection the revelers will taste? They won't be able to say what it is, but they will never have eaten anything so delicious in their lives." He looked at me almost like he was proud of me. "Can you stay like this, my sweet? If you can stay like this, you will be rewarded with a feast of feasts."

"Yes..." I wouldn't really know unless I tried, would I? At any rate, I wasn't moving until he chose to free me.

He went back to his work, and I watched him peel chestnuts and boil them with milk and mash them into a paste, finally whipping them with cocoa powder and sugar into a warm brown, lustrous filling for little baked pastry cups. A different cream, flavored with cinnamon and sweet wine, filled chocolates. Little tarts received a daub of quince jam before he crimped them shut. And then, there were cakes, with layers of frosting of different flavors and colors.

I'm not sure how he produced all this in one night, nor

how I stayed there to watch all that time. There was magic in this place, that was sure. I loved watching him; the speed and skill with which he created these astonishing confections. I had never been so stimulated, by all the smells of chocolate, baking pastry, spices and simmering cream, the blasts of warm air that brushed my bare skin when he opened the oven door, and most of all, the way he watched me in return. I fueled his work. I had only known him for this short time, but I could already tell he had more energy as the night went on. His pale skin seemed to take on a faint glow.

If my desire for him started to wane in the least, he would walk over to me briskly. The first time he did this, suddenly crossing the room toward me without warning, I held my breath. He touched the wand to my clit and flicked it back and forth across the tender nub until I moaned. I was wet again in no time, and he took another taste, and then resumed what he was doing.

We didn't speak much that night. He had never told me not to speak, and I don't think he would have scolded me if I had, but it felt like the spell cast on us would be broken. Our understanding of one another was taking shape without words.

Then, as the sun was rising, I heard horses.

Alarm flickered across his face before he regained calm. He quickly freed me from my bonds, so quickly that I stumbled out of them. He yanked a curtain across to hide the rack. "Get in the pantry," he said, pointing at the narrow door, "and hide there. Don't make a sound until I tell you."

This was no time for questions. I rushed toward the door on legs that were a little shaky from being caught in the same position for so long and shut myself in the dark room, kneeling on the hard stone floor. I knew the room well already; I had been watching him take things in and out all night.

I heard a knock on the door and the Magus answered in a smooth voice. "Good morning, King Will. This is a surprise."

"Is it? Just a routine inspection. I pay them to everyone."

"Yes, you are very thorough with maintenance, I've noticed."

"Spare me," said King Will. *The King of the Revels?* I wondered. "I just want to look in on the operations." His voice was drawing closer now as he came through the door to the kitchens. "I know very well that when *you* were the King of the Revels, maintenance and inspections were the last thing on *your* mind."

At first I wondered if he misspoke, but the Magus didn't correct him.

"Are you really going to mock me for insufficient inspections? *Human*," the Magus said, scornfully. "You'll always be a human, even if your eyes turn gold, even if you speak to my trees."

"And you will always be a exile," King Will replied, not backing down in the least.

"I wouldn't get too cocky. Many of my people have trouble stomaching a human in charge."

"I'm here because 'your' people put me there. Even when your sentence ends, you're not welcome in court."

The revelation struck me like lightning. The Magus used to be a Faery King...now he was merely the baker of the court. Why had he been exiled?

Why would the faeries exile the Magus and instill a human king? I needed to find out.

# Chapter Five

GRETEL

KING WILL and the Magus exchanged a few more barbs before he left and the pantry door opened.

"You're free now," he said. "You are permitted to put your clothes on and have your feast."

My eyes must have been full of questions, but I chose one first. "You used to be the King of the Wicked Revels?"

"Yes."

"Can you tell me what happened?"

"Some of it. Over dinner."

I pulled on my shift and plain dress. He set the table with another beautiful meal. When Hansel was here, I was still a little too nervous to eat my fill, but now I could hardly help myself. The leg of lamb was so savory that I had to keep reminding myself not to shovel it in my mouth like a boor.

I think he drank more wine than ate. He seemed agitated, his fingers twisting together. "Gretel," he said.

"When I was the King of the Wicked Revels, I made some serious mistakes. Despite my bitterness over being usurped, it's a truth I can't deny."

"What sort of mistakes? Isn't the Wicked Revels mainly just a dance?"

"The Wicked Revels is much more than a dance. It's a place to explore all of one's desires. But it is also supposed to be safe. As the king, it was my job to make sure that no one felt like they might be taken advantage of. After I claimed the throne, I was so happy to be free that I failed in my duty. I didn't oversee my guards as I should, and they were spending more time flirting than watching over the dance. A rogue faery man arrived at the revels and raped several of the girls. At the subsequent council where the girls attested to his crimes before me...I couldn't bear the fear and hurt on their faces. I had failed them. What should have been a place of pleasure and security had now given them a pain to carry all their lives."

"Oh, Magus..."

He shook his head. "My attempt to correct that tragedy only made it worse. I used my magic to create a new rule. All the girls would be given masks to wear, created from a piece of wood from the oldest tree in the forest, and as long as they wore a mask, no man could touch them in a sexual way, not even me. They had to give up their mask to a man first. They had to consent not just with words but with deeds, baring to him what had been hidden. It worked quite well..." He took a long swig of his drink. "...at first. Magic has a tendency to produce unforeseen consequences."

"What happened then?" I asked. He looked very pale again.

"The act of the girls turning over the mask to the men they loved became a magical pledge as strong as a marriage vow between them. And *I* cast the original spell. *I* created the bond between the tree and the masks. So I ended up picking up on the magical energy of their unions. All of them. No girl ever offered me her mask. In many ways, I didn't truly want a mask or a wife. I didn't want to give up the thrill of the chase. In a literal sense, I have never lain with a woman, believe it or not, but I sensed every pairing that happened under my watch, felt every pleasure as if it were my own, and in that sense hardly a moment went by when I was not awash in seduction. It was powerful magic, a drug to me and the main source of my power. It was hard, then, for me not to start interfering in the lives of my subjects, wanting them to join and push each other to new heights of pleasure. But...that isn't what the Wicked Revels were about. They weren't free anymore if I was controlling them."

"And so...that was why they overthrew you?"

"Yes. I wooed the Princess Evaline of Torina, and that man who is now king snuck into the Revels and fell in love with her." He frowned, silent for a time. "We fought over her as men do. But...some of my people encouraged Will to defeat me for good. I was drunk on the power of my own magic and rather than discuss it with me, they wanted me gone."

"It is hard to *discuss* things with a king," I said.

"I wasn't the sort of king who put people in dungeons for arguing with me," he said crossly. "But nevermind that. I was banished from the Revels. The masks have been abolished. King Will and Queen Evaline keep with the old rules, where the guards watch over the dancers and the people protect each other. It is only through the sacrifice and loyalty of my old baker Aramy that I am here in any capacity. But I am not allowed to see the festivities that were once my home. Will doesn't trust me. He thought I was dead. If I wanted to remain in this realm, he sentenced me not to touch a woman, nor bring her pleasure, for three years—and banned me from the Wicked Revels for life."

"Why didn't you just...leave the realm?"

"This is my home. I won't be run out of it by a human. I have no hope of happiness anywhere else."

"So it's because of Will that you can't touch me. But how much of those three years have passed? Won't you be able to touch again very soon?"

"Another curse was placed upon me," the Magus said. "And that has nothing to do with Will. I can't speak of it."

"This curse...it means you won't be able to touch me even when the three years are up?"

He paused. "That is one consequence, yes."

"What else?"

"I can't say."

I realized this was something I could only find out on my own, so I changed subjects. "You said your old baker saved you. How did you end up as the baker?"

"Aramy offered me his job and taught me his trade, so I could stay here. It was the only way. The artisans of the Revels have the right to appoint their successors. Otherwise Will would have nothing to do with me." He shoved his plate back, still half full of food. "It's ridiculous. I am not a baker."

"You seem quite good at it, though," I said. "And don't tell me you don't enjoy it. I watched you all day." I picked up his plate, almost out of habit, like I was cleaning the table after giving Hansel his dinner. "Why don't you give me a taste of what you made today and I'll tell you if you're a baker or not?"

"You don't have to clean up after me, my Gretel. That isn't what you're here for."

"I don't mind. I like moving around after a long day of...not doing much at all."

He acquiesced. As I cleared the plates and took them to the sink, he went to the front room where all the cakes and sweets were laid out on the table. I kept passing him as I went back and forth. He selected a few of the small sweets and put them on a plate, and after I washed the dishes, they were waiting for me.

"Take them to bed if you like," he said. "I need some sleep myself. But Gretel?"

"Yes?"

"Don't touch yourself. I will know. The taste of the chocolate will have to bear the weight of all your desires."

# Chapter Six

❦

GRETEL

I WAS INDEED, very aroused, but also very tired, so I had no trouble following his rules. I wondered if he would make me stay bound up all day once again. The idea still made my body terribly excited but my mind dreaded another day of being idle. I wanted to get my hands on the all his beautiful ingredients.

When I came downstairs in the morning, the rack was still behind a curtain, and after making a quick breakfast that we ate in the kitchen, he gave me a paper box. I could feel the gentle weight of fabric inside.

"I want you to take your clothes off and put these on," he said. "And then I believe you might like to help me in the kitchen."

"You believe correctly, sir!"

"So enthusiastic," he said, with a faint smile.

I opened the box. The first was a black ribbon choker with a pale blue stone at my throat. I hooked the clasp at the back of my neck, knowing it would show off my bare neck very well with my braids wound at the crown of my head. Next, the dress—I pulled it out and my stomach dipped when I saw what was beneath it, but that would wait. The gown was storm-blue, and the fabric was almost sheer. When I pulled off my sturdy wool and linen garments and put the dress on, it was like wearing cobwebs and clouds. It was sleeveless and clingy, in a silky way that moved with me. It barely covered my torso and back. The skirt had several long layers, but they were all thin, and all the outlines of my body remained visible.

"Very good," he said. "I want to see you."

His voice had a possessive note that drove me halfway to madness already. I don't know why I wanted so much for him to want to see me, but it was not mere flattery. I didn't feel like I was just a pretty girl for him. What had he said? *Pleasure is its own sort of art.* That was how I felt, like he was turning me into art. Not something merely pretty, but something a little bit uncomfortable. Something that made us both confront ourselves in different ways.

Finally, there was the last bit. A sort of undergarment made of supple leather, with a stiff wooden phallus jutting out on the inside. It was the same sort of soft, living wood that the bonds on the rack were made out of. I wondered if he could make the phallus move with the tap of his wand, the way the bonds open and shut.

I hesitated although I was so wet I certainly would have no trouble putting it on. Perhaps my hesitation was simply that it ashamed me how eager I was and that he could see that eagerness. Or maybe it was because I was dreaming of being fucked by that thing until I reached my peak, and I knew this was not what would happen. He had already made that clear.

"Go on, Gretel. We have a lot of work to do."

I stepped into the undergarment and drew it up my legs until the phallus touched my entrance. Now I had to reach down and guide it in. I'd stroked my inner passage with my fingers before but never anything so large as this. I was so slick there that it wasn't as much trouble as I would expect, but the feeling was intense as it stretched and filled me like nothing ever had before. I was already so aroused that the single stroke of pushing it past my inner walls made me moan. It felt as smooth as glass—and as hard, too, the length of it unyielding inside me. I clutched the table with my free hand.

"Look at me," he said, when I shut my eyes and dropped my head.

I bit my lip, forcing my eyes upward.

"I regret that I can only offer you something inanimate," he said. "Does it brush your sweet spot inside?"

"Ahh...maybe...almost." As I forced the last inch inside me, I felt something like a fingertip brushing across a spot of hot pleasure, not unlike my clit, but deep inside. It was only a fluttering touch. I wanted to scream for more.

"Almost is exactly the right answer," he said. He tapped the edges of the soft leather around my pussy with the wand, checking to see that it fit, I suppose. "Now, I am going to shift the wood a bit. You should also feel a slight pressure on your clit," he said. He stroked the wand across the leather right where my clit was, and I felt two small, precise pieces of wood slide up to hug my swollen bud, like two fingers gently pinching me there. In both cases I felt like someone was touching me, faintly. Testing me. Teasing at my desire.

It was subtle, and subtle was more cruel than anything. My heart was pounding. My inner walls clenched against the firm intrusion inside them. I couldn't help it; I stroked my hand along my clit, trying to stimulate myself through the leather. I wanted a firmer touch.

He flicked the wand at my hand, producing a sharp brief snap of pain. "You know the bargain, Gretel."

"I can't bear it."

"You will learn to bear it. Look at my cock." His manhood was a cruel, swollen length from watching me. "I would give anything to touch you right now, but…if you really do want to save me, this is our only hope. My magic must be pushed to the limit."

"What will that do?"

"Every day you're here, as your desire builds, my magic grows stronger and the confections I make for the Wicked Revels will be more and more delicious. Currently, the king and queen would love to get rid of me. But the more you're begging to be satisfied, the more delicious the cake will taste. Magic feeds on sacrifice."

"Are you sure you're not just repeating your old mistake in a different way? Feeding on desire, like with the masks?"

"No," he said. "This is why I asked your permission explicitly. Before, I was feeding on *all* of my subjects and they didn't even know. I have no wish to do that anymore. I am just drawing magic from you. We have spoken the right words to each other and there is no deception. If I fail this time, that will be the end. If I succeed, I will have you and only you."

"I see."

"Do you regret giving your permission?"

I wanted him so badly that it was unbearable, but I knew I would bear it. A part of me relished it. In the end, I felt sure I would be satisfied so fully that every moment of this would be worth it. "No…"

"If you start to feel yourself tipping forward into satisfaction, you will tell me," he said. "So I can stop you."

"Yes....," I said, the word wringing out of me.

"Now, we're going to work and you have to try and focus, because the court expects the finest, every night. Since you have such a fine eye for detail, and careful hands, I wonder if you could make me some decorations of marzipan to top the cakes?"

"Oh, yes!"

I would never have been able to buy such things. He offered me several rolls of marzipan wrapped in paper with a band of gold foil around them with a picture that said "Gloss Family Confections, Serving the Royal Families for 250 Years". The shops in Aupenburg did not even sell such things, needless to say. I had an array of colorings to work into the marzipan, in the warm shades of berry juices and flower petals, and immediately I started coloring and forming the paste into shapes.

"How many cakes are you making?" I asked.

"Just three today."

"What do you think of each cake having a theme with tiny little marzipan figures? One could be a mother bird feeding her little ones, one a farmyard with chickens and pigs, one a unicorn in a grove of flowers."

"Do you think you can manage all that on your first try?"

"I don't know, but is there any harm in the attempt?"

"Start with the farmyard," he said. "See how you do."

While I shaped marzipan, he mixed the cake batter. Whenever I moved, I was teased with little bits of stimulation. Even staying perfectly still, I felt a faint pressure on my clit, and if I considered it too much, I started feeling like I was on fire, my core throbbing with desire. His presence alone always provided an additional stirring. He was so handsome, so confident as he worked that I would never know he hadn't been a baker since childhood. The fact that he could not tell me everything mirrored the fact that he couldn't touch me. I wondered if there was *anyone* who could tell me the full story.

I kept my hands very busy and tried my best not to think of it. Now that I was working with him, we talked a little more, although he seemed reluctant to engage in any substantial conversation.

"I don't know if I should speak of the Wicked Revels when I can't bring you to the dance," he said.

"I am happy just to be here, but I want to know what happens there. How did you become the king? Were you born there?"

"No, actually. That may have been why I didn't manage it as I should. I grew up in more of an ordinary faery court."

"What does an ordinary faery court look like?"

"To a human, maybe not that ordinary. Where do I even begin?" His attention seemed to drift into memory. "No, it wasn't ordinary, after all."

"Tell me about it."

"I am from the court of Ellurine." The name rolled off his tongue like it had a life of its own. "Have you heard of it?"

"No. But I'm only a farm girl." I lifted my eyebrows.

"Why do you do that, Gretel? Claim to be only a farm girl? You know you are more than that now."

"They would think me...less than that now," I stammered. I guess deep down, I was like Hansel after all, worrying I had done something wrong.

The Magus scoffed. "Own what you are, my dear." He continued, "As a child, I didn't have any proper lessons. Faery children there can spend their days running wild. Nothing is considered naughty unless irreparable damage is done."

"So nothing we're doing now is naughty, is it?"

That almost got a smile out of him. "Not to me. However..." He spooned honey out of a stone crock. "When you come of age, everything changes. At that point, Ellurine becomes a theater, where everyone has a costume and a role. Lines to speak. Actions to perform. Once your role is decided, that is who you will be forever. You take the role from someone else, and when you die, it goes on to the next."

"That sounds strict."

"Every court in the world has some version of it," he said. "Every king is just playing a role. But yes, in Ellurine it goes much farther. It isn't just kings and queens, but the entire court. There are several ministers whose sole job is to counsel everyone on their roles and quietly remove those who can't conform. Some people dream of attaining one of these coveted roles, but I was horrified of it."

"I can see why! But you didn't stay in Ellurine. Now I understand why you said you felt so free at the Revels."

"Yes," he said, snapping the spoon against the rim of the bowl. The honey slid slowly into a pool of melted butter. "That life would have broken me. My nephew Deniel is next in line for the throne now, and he's wrestling with the burden. I don't envy him."

"How did you end up leading the Wicked Revels, then?"

"The King of the Wicked Revels at that time was my father's cousin, Llynfar. I begged him to appoint me as his heir so I could escape Ellurine. And he did. When Llynfar died, he left the Revels to me. I was—so he said—the correct mix of responsible and wild. You don't want the King of the Revels to be *too* responsible."

"Will is too responsible, isn't he?"

"I dare not comment on what I think of Will." He beat a bowl of batter with vigor.

But King Will certainly must have liked the desserts from last night. His coach came riding up to the cottage again before nightfall, and once again I hid in the pantry.

"I don't know what you did last night, but do it again," he said. His voice, compared to the Magus' low liquid growl, was plain and direct. "And make more if you can. Everything was gone before the first jig."

"I'll try. I can only make so much. Hopefully the ones I have made today will do."

"These are rather whimsical," Will said, with some surprise. He must have been looking at my marzipan decorations. "I didn't take you for having much...whimsy."

"Well." It was a shrug of a word. "Enjoy them."

I heard Will's footsteps move—it sounded like he had a bad leg. Then stop. "Are you up to something, Magus?"

"New recipes."

"Are you alone here?"

"Ah, Will, faeries cannot lie. I'm never alone. There are always mice in this cottage despite my best efforts to discourage them."

"Not in the cake, I hope."

"Never."

Soon the pantry door swung open. "You've done very well, Gretel, in ways I didn't expect. It's as if your decorations for the cakes complement the magic you've given me with a visual."

"I seem to be making Will suspicious."

"You are. It doesn't matter. He likes the food too much to push any farther. He tasted the magic. No one is immune to the charms."

I couldn't help but think the Magus was being a bit wicked, despite his protests, but I didn't say anything. "I enjoyed doing it," I said, hoping this meant I could become a regular part of the shop.

He fed me another glorious meal; the food seemed to appear like magic. Before I went to bed, he said, "You can take off your panties now.".

Despite the constant teasing of it, I hated to remove them too, because I would feel so empty. The phallus was like a proxy for him. It was coated with the wetness that had been trickling out of me all day.

"Remember, Gretel, don't touch yourself." He said this like they were magic words.

"I won't."

But as the days went on, it was almost impossible to resist.

# Chapter Seven

GRETEL

I SURVIVED it for almost two weeks. Two weeks! I had agreed to survive it forever, but how could I do such a thing? I must not have known how long forever was. No one could survive this, I told myself. The shape of the phallus and the wooden fingers gently pinching my clit changed a little every day, as if to provide a slightly new experience and new surprise every day, so I was never offered the relief of being dulled to the sensation. A part of me was always on the edge of losing my mind.

But I could not lose my mind, because I finally had work worthy of my talents and interests. I would have aspired to be a baker long ago if I'd known, I thought. I sprinkled poppy seeds on little twists of pastry. I painstakingly decorated two hundred chocolates with a star pattern made of almond shards. I cut candied orange peels into long strips and draped them on tiny honey cakes. I iced cakes and covered them in patterns of drizzled icing and shavings of chocolate or rings of different colored berries. I made everything look beautiful and I took pride in doing it.

And I was getting to know him better, liking him more every day. We worked so well together, and it suited me. We fell into patterns of understanding, turning out our sweets like parts of a clockwork. We could go hours without speaking, but it never felt strange. I felt like I was home. When we did speak, slowly peeling back the layers of ourselves, I realized I had finally found the person who understood me.

One morning I woke to find I was fondling myself in my sleep. I snapped my hand away, but it felt so wonderful. I wanted more. I let my hands drift to my breasts instead, trying to soothe away the ache of desire with something gentler.

It was no use. Would he really know if I touched myself just for a few moments? Just a moment... All the fantasies of things I wished for the Magus to do to me sprang to mind immediately and I was half-lost in it. Before I knew it, I felt a tingling pulse that signaled I was growing very close, and this frightened me enough to stop. I dragged myself out of bed.

*I can't hold out. I just can't. There seems no end to this waiting. I need his touch. Or at least I need* someone's *touch, even my own! What can I do?* Whenever anyone came to the cottage to pick up the sweets, he made me hide. Maybe I just had to keep waiting, but he couldn't tell me if or when I would ever get what I wanted.

*I can't keep waiting. But what could I do, leave him?*

When I saw him that morning, I feared he would know I had been weak. He gave no sign of that, however. We had breakfast as usual, but I was agitated. Electrified with wanting.

We went to the workroom and it was the same as every other morning, but when the slivers of wood hugged my clit, my body started pulsing urgently. I was so heated that even this insufficient touch was going to push me too far. My brain raced for a moment. *I need to tell him I'm too close.*

I simply couldn't make myself say the words. I turned to a bowl of strawberries that needed trimming but my inner walls clamped against the phallus and I was flexing against that firm length and seeing stars. I made an involuntary gasp. Suddenly I was coming and I couldn't stop it. I knew I shouldn't let this happen, if I had any choice, but it was the most glorious sensation I could imagine. I was shattering, the feelings radiating all the way to my fingers and toes. I leaned on the table, making quick and anguished breaths, as heat convulsed through me. My knees sagged. The relief of it!

"Gretel!" he barked.

"Please—I can't—" I was sobbing as it passed through me. "It's too much. I've failed you. I—I—"

"Why didn't you tell me you were so close?"

"I couldn't! I needed this!"

"You know what I asked of you!"

"I know, but—"

He lifted my skirt and spanked my ass hard several times. This only seemed to intensify the final waves of my orgasm. I bowed forward onto the table, flour smudging my face and hands, craving more of his precious touch.

He hissed, pulling back. His palm was an angry red.

"Curses!" He raged, kicking over a butter churn. "Curses on all of them. Damn King Will, damn my court, damn that ugly goblin, damn *me*."

"Ugly goblin? What goblin?"

"Damn you too." He pounded his fists on the table.

I was a little more myself now and as the haze lifted I

realized that he might have to send me away now. I straightened up slowly. The dread of it made me feel heavy. I didn't know where I would go if I couldn't be here. It was impossible, the idea of leaving him. Utterly impossible. "Magus—"

"Take off your clothes and get on the rack."

I obeyed him quickly and my relief seemed so short lived. As he tapped the restraints with his wand and they closed around my wrists and ankles, I thought I was more aroused than ever. I started crying. My tears sounded rather angry in my frustration.

He unbuttoned his trousers and took out his stiff cock. I went silent at the sight of it. Only my pussy wept now.

"Please," I whispered, although looking at his hand, I knew he could do nothing.

He put his burnt hand on the wall behind me, and stroked his cock with his other hand, so close that I could feel the warmth of his body. His hand slid faster and faster along his thick length, and I moaned, just thinking about how it would feel to touch him, to have him inside me, warm and living. I knew we would find the perfect rhythm, just as we did when we worked together.

"Gretel." His voice was rough. "If you've ruined this, it's only fair we both enjoy it." He started spilling his seed so fast that I knew he had shared all my desire. The hot liquid hit my bare stomach as he breathed quick, with an unbidden, anguished growl at the back of it all.

He looked immediately healthier, with more color in his face. Stripped of his royal title, I thought, he was just the Magus. And this was his magic. Not healing or creating fire or bottling up curses, like an ordinary mage. Pleasure was his currency, and without it, he was as poor and starved as I had ever been.

He searched my face. "I want to dry your tears," he

said. "I wish I could touch you. I wish I could...show you how I feel for you. You understand me, don't you?"

"I do."

"I've been given a sentence and I've been given a curse. Together, they have made my fate impossible."

I thought about this for a moment—a sentence, and a curse. "King Will sentenced you not to touch me. Is the ugly goblin the one who cursed you, then?"

"I can't speak of the curse. That is the first rule of curses, Gretel." He shut his eyes for a moment, and pulled back from me. "The King of the Wicked Revels is supposed to tease out one's hidden desires. Not force something unwanted. If this is too much for you and you want to go, Gretel, you may go."

"I *don't* want to go!"

He laughed dryly. "You really don't, do you? You are truly my match. You don't shrink from anything I do to you."

"Do I have to go? Did I ruin everything?"

"Maybe not. I can attempt to dispel the energy. Wait here."

"*Right* here?" I squirmed in my bonds.

"You deserve a little punishment, don't you think? I will be back soon."

"How soon?"

He walked out the door without answering me.

# Chapter Eight

THE MAGUS

I HAD BEEN a dead man for almost three years now, but before I stalked out the door, I caught a glimpse of my face in the mirror and saw a little color in my cheeks.

*She could bring me back to life.*

But my situation was brutal and impossible. Aramy should have known better than to treat with such a man as the Trickster Mage. Night after night, I ran that fateful morning over in my mind.

*Please, my lord, can you hear me? You're alive. Thank the gods.* Aramy's voice had reached through the fog. I woke from the worst dream of my life, and then I realized that maybe it wasn't a dream.

His relief matched my dread. *I was dead,* I said. *Will killed me. I'm sure of it.* I could still feel the knife in my back. *What did you do?*

*I asked the Trickster Mage for a favor, my lord. He pulled you back from the brink of the underworld.*

*What? What have you done? The Trickster never offers a good bargain.*

*My first born.* Aramy had laughed. *First born? At my age? The joke's on him. Now, there is a stipulation, but at least you have time. You must join with a girl who loves you as you love her within three years.*

*So I have to live in this world where my position has been usurped by a human?*

*My lord, the kingdom still needs you. Many are loyal to you, even though they're quiet now. Be patient and you might have your throne back. I was already planning to retire, help my brother out with the flour mill. I'll show you how to make the confections for the Wicked Revels.*

Until now, I wished my loyal baker had left me for dead. As soon as I returned to the Wicked Revels, I had to see my rival on my throne, and when he condemned me not to a touch a woman for three years, I knew that the Trickster Mage had foreseen this all along.

But I had Gretel now.

Since I lost my throne, my thoughts had been consumed by bitterness, but now they were consumed with thoughts of her face. When we parted for each night, I could hardly wait for the next day, to work alongside her. I had never dreamed of taking on a trade, but Gretel was born to put her mind and hands to work. She loved to make humble things beautiful. Her face was aglow when she iced a cake. In this, we were different.

But in other matters, we were the same. For years now, I had been leading human girls to the Wicked Revels, but I had never met one like Gretel. I realized now why I had always failed to seal the deal with girls in the past. The others could never keep up with me. To other humans, sex was a pleasure and a shame, but to Gretel, it was an art and a way of life, a journey into the depths of her psyche. I could tell she liked that it was never far from her mind, that she was in a constant state of being stirred. She would have been able to handle this agonizing tease, I thought, if only I could assure her this exquisite torture had a proper end. What made her weak this morning was that I couldn't promise anything.

I had to promise she would be mine at the end of it all, and I had to fulfill that promise.

First things first.

The magical energy of our climax this morning would be something any King of the Revels would sense, even that damned human Will. I had to cleanse the house before anyone picked up on it, or my game would be exposed. Will would search the house, find Gretel, and take her from me.

I walked as briskly down the forest paths as I could without breaking into a run, all the way to Marte's cottage, and pounded on the door.

Marte was one I could still trust. She had criticized my handling of the Revels quite a few times, but she also had little love for humans.

Her house was built into a hollow hill, the windows cut into the grass. The door creaked open. "And what brings you here to see me, Sir Magus?"

Coming from my own people, the title chafed. They gave me some honor by calling me a Magus and not merely a baker, but once, I was "your highness" and "your majesty". Of course, I was the one who I refused to be called by my name. I had always been a man with a title, not a name. "I need a dispelling spell."

"Dispelling spell?" She hissed out the "s" sounds with amusement. "Aramy says you have a lady with you."

"Aramy would probably do well not to talk about my business," I growled.

"Indeed. Trust is one of his faults. We know that. The lad made some sort of bargain to get you back, after all!" She laughed. Aramy was no lad at ninety years old, but Marte was older still. She waved me in and glanced at my hand. "Do you need healing balm as well? You must have touched something you oughtn't. Any other...appendages that need attending?"

"No." I was not in the mood for Marte's sense of humor. "The girl was the one who failed to stick to the terms of my sentence."

"Well..." Marte glanced me over. "That, I can believe. If you decided you had a taste for old women, I would not stick to the terms either."

Damnit, she almost got a chuckle out of me. "Just give me the spell." Following her through the dim rooms, I had to hastily duck not to hit my head on a beam.

"I have something else you might make use of. Well, well, I haven't used this one in a while." I didn't really want to think about the zest in her tone when she said this. It was obvious that when Marte said "used" she didn't mean "gave to someone else". She pulled a bottle off a cluttered shelf, brushing cobwebs away with her hand. "This gives your lover more stamina."

"As in...?"

"It will take much longer, and much more intense stimulation, for her to climax. No more accidents, hm? This is important. You can't have Will sensing what you're up to before your sentence is over, can you?"

"No..."

"I hear talk, Magus," she said. "The people would kill for a taste of those cakes and sweets of yours, you know." Her eyes twinkled. "They might kill any man who would take you away from them, too. Perhaps it's good for every king to take a stint as an artisan."

"Perhaps," I said, with a small bow. She was giving me a signal. She would support me if I took back the throne. She felt I had learned my lesson. I was the only one who could give my people what they needed.

Time was running short. I had to hope that the magic infused within the cakes was working on my people, and even the ones who had once rebelled against me would support me now. I could only join with Gretel unless Will was out of the way, with his own inherited magic broken. It was hard not to feel pessimistic. I couldn't tell anyone the exact nature of the curse. Even Marte had no idea how dire my situation really was.

Despite it all, I could not suppress a thrill of anticipation when I took the spell. If what Marte said was true, I could up the ante with Gretel, and my magic would grow stronger still. She would scream, she would writhe, she would beg me for mercy, but I knew she would never tell me to stop.

# Chapter Nine

GRETEL

I WAS in unbearable anticipation for his return, my legs spread and waiting for him. I was never in pain when I was bound by him; some magic was certainly at work. The faery world seemed to have so many tricks for making my wildest fantasies come true; not just that I was tied up by a beautiful man, but that I could withstand it for so long. I felt sure that if I was back in the human world, this would not feel so delicious. But what did I care for the human world anymore?

When I heard the door unlock and open, I strained at my bonds. But then my stomach dropped. I knew the Magus' footsteps. This was a stranger. And here I was, naked and spread and wet.

"Please," I whispered to the wooden restraints. "Please let me go!" I tugged at them. The whole rack rattled. I managed to jiggle my arms and legs down into a slightly less prone position and that was the best I could do.

"Magus...?" An unfamiliar male voice sang out the word through the doorway before he appeared. I heard the tap of a cane—or a magical staff, in fact, as he entered the room.

*A goblin.*

I had never seen a goblin up close. They never came through Aupenburg. Some goblins liked to trade with humans, and others stole things, but our village was too poor for either kind to bother.

He was every bit as alarming as I could imagine, a rangy figure with impressively clawed hands. I could barely see his eyes through a tangle of thick black hair that brushed his shoulders, but that made his fearsome teeth all the more visible. He had two black horns reaching straight up from his head, shaped almost like the perked ears of a wolf.

"Well, well...what have we here?" he asked, in a slightly raspy voice. "The Magus appears to be doing well for himself. A flaxen-haired beauty hung up to dry... Something to eat over the winter?"

"N-no," I sputtered. I had no idea if he was joking. He poked me with the tip of his wooden staff and tears sprang to my eyes. My instincts had told me I could trust the Magus from my first sight of him. They were telling me the opposite now. "Please—he'll be back any moment."

"Don't worry a hair on your head. I don't bother with this sort of thing." He flicked a dismissive hand at my naked body. "Nothing makes men weak like love, does it?" He plucked a freshly baked pastry off the counter and popped it in his mouth. "Mm-*hm*," he said, an approving critique.

"Then what are you here for?"

"He only has four weeks left, your Magus."

"Four weeks of the three years of his sentence?"

"Four weeks of the three years of my curse."

"You're—"

"The Trickster Mage, they call *me*." He grinned at me, and I could only see the faint glint of one eye through his hair. He ate another pastry. "And as Mages go, I'm one of the best. I brought him back to life, did he tell you that?"

"No..."

"No, he can't, can he? Those were part of my terms. I don't really like to spread the word that I bring people back from the dead."

He frightened me, this strange mage. Maybe this was how Hansel felt around *my* Magus. I was in the presence of something I didn't really understand, but this was the ugly goblin who had placed the curse, that was clear. He must have come for a reason. "Sir...Trickster Mage, please...is there any way I can break your curse?"

"You could give me your firstborn child."

"No!" I said reflexively. Any happiness the Magus and I might find would be short lived if we had to give away our first child.

"You could guess my name."

"Guess your name?"

"I'll give you three chances."

"But...I haven't the slightest idea."

He shrugged his slender shoulders. He was wearing a loose patchwork coat that fell almost to the tops of his tall black boots, and no shirt beneath it, just pale skin with a few scars, and several pendants hanging around his neck. "Not even a guess?"

"Uh...Jack?"

He laughed. "No."

"Puck?"

"No."

"Robin?"

He laughed. "I have heard worse attempts. But, no. Shall I tell you my bargain with the Magus? You won't be able to tell anyone else, but perhaps you will reconsider what you're willing to sacrifice."

"I'm not giving you any of my children," I said. "Maybe you had better just leave." Even if he wasn't interested in me, I didn't like unsettling company, especially in this state.

"She tries to hide her fear," he murmured. "And I admire the effort. Your Magus must join with someone who loves him by Samhain night, you know. I thought it was a pretty easy thing to ask of a man so charming..."

*But he can't touch anyone.* It was immediately clear to me what the Magus meant by a sentence and a curse. Will sentenced him not to touch anyone for three years. The Trickster Mage cursed him so that he *had* to touch someone within three years.

*And he can't tell Will what his curse is...*

"I suppose I can leave you to ponder that," the Trickster Mage said. "I will leave you be. But do tell him I stopped by."

"I will." I bowed my head in good-bye, and he left, thank *heavens*.

The Magus returned a little later, and he seemed pleased. He put two bottles on the work table and opened a tall one with a slender neck. A plume of smoke emerged from the opening and he carried the bottle around the room, cutting his wand through the smoky ribbon to disperse the magic.

"So you got the spell?" I asked.

"Yes, my dear. A truly astute king might sense around it, which is why we must not make any more mistakes, but Will is green."

By now, I'd had a little time to consider this curse. "Do you truly want to deceive Will?"

He lifted a brow. "I must, Gretel. Otherwise he would send me away."

"I just wonder if...Will could be obliged to lift your sentence early."

"I have no interested in begging to Will."

"I understand that you're proud, but you did admit yourself that you made mistakes as king. And I can't help but wonder if—"

"If?" He walked up close to me. He smelled, faintly, of magic. I'm not sure I had ever smelled magic before, but I knew it: smoky and green, like every season at once.

I held my ground, despite my compromising position, meeting his eyes. "Can you please set me free so we can talk?"

"No, I'd like to hear this right away."

"Have you *ever* tried to talk to Will?"

"Talking is impossible. Will despises me and I despise him."

"You're manipulating Will and the Revelers again," I said. "Using magic that comes from me to win back their favor." I struggled against my shackles. "I've never seen the Revels. I don't know what they were like when you were king, and I don't know what they're like now. But you're banned from them too. Is it possible that Will isn't such a terrible king at all, and this is just a misunderstanding?"

He paused. As well as we got along, we had never argued. I expected him to dismiss my suggestion, as Hansel would. I braced for a fight. I could feel my stomach muscles clenching up with dread.

But the Magus was as cool as Hansel was hot-tempered.

"I don't want to make the same mistakes," he said. "All I really want is you. But I'm not going to *beg* Will to lift my sentence. Will is ruling my people like a human king. He wants rules and order. He doesn't understand the revels and he never will. I don't need to see his Revels. I can guess what it's like. They're supposed to be the grandest party in the realm."

"Do you think I would understand the revels?"

"You? Oh, yes."

"I'm human."

"You're no ordinary human." He paused. "Who was here?" he asked me.

"The Trickster Mage. He told me about your curse. He told me—you will die on Samhain night if we don't make love!"

He took a slow breath. "I have a plan."

"And what is that?"

"To usurp Will. Aramy is gathering faery clans who are loyal to me, including my nephew's forces back in Ellurine. On Samhain night, we will run the humans out."

"But—"

"I don't want to hurt them," he said. "I just want them to go back where they belong. And you would be my queen, the queen of the most joyous throne in all the realm."

Dismay shot through me. I couldn't help but wonder if he was really meant to be king. But I knew him as a baker. This was the life I loved. I didn't want things to change, and maybe that was my own mistake. I wasn't sure what to say. Something about all of this just didn't feel right.

He picked up a cask of the weak, sweet faery wine that we sometimes drank during the day. "You must be thirsty." He opened the other bottle and put a drop of honey-colored liquid in the wine.

"What is that?"

"You don't want to be surprised?"

"If it's an aphrodisiac...I really don't need it."

He laughed. "No, no. If you really want to know, it makes you last longer before you climax. It will keep you safe until Samhain. And I want you to take it. There are even more things we can do, with this."

I could not even help wetting my lips.

"Gretel, I swear to you...I *will* break the spell and make all our suffering worth it. You will be my queen and I will love you until the end of our days, in the way you deserve." He held the cup to my lips, carefully. I drank, some of it dribbling down my chin. He grabbed his apron, which was draped on the table, and wiped it off me, sucking a little air between his teeth at the contact of his hand through layers of fabric. He had said he could not even touch me through a glove.

"I want to do things a little differently now," he said. "Not a moment will go by when you aren't thinking about how much you want my cock inside you, from now until the moment I finally claim you for my own."

My breath hitched with desire as his words seemed to melt in my ears like chocolate melting on my tongue. If I had not been bound I think I would have had to touch his face and burn him. "Magus...that sounds no different at all."

"It will be different. It will be worse. Even at night, I want you to wear your panties, and I want you to sleep in my bed. And if I should hear you stir, I might just brush my wand against your pussy and change the shape a little so you are penetrated even deeper than before and you will yearn for me always. Would you like that, Gretel?"

A moan dragged out of me. "Magus, please..."

"As I thought." He freed my feet from the shackles and took the undergarment, sliding it up my legs, careful not to touch my skin. The thick phallus slid into me easily, slick as I was. He tapped the wand and it seemed to turn almost liquid inside me, but still firm, shifting shape back and forth. I don't think it could change volume, so the wood changed from thick and short to long and narrow, quickly, with each rapid tap of the wand. The effect was an unpredictable, rapid penetration that tore a scream of pleasure out of me almost instantly. My feet found the ground and scrabbled back and forth. I don't know if I was trying to escape the sensation or draw it in deeper.

"Magus, please...!" I screamed again.

He stopped with a wicked grin. My core was so hot, all my small muscles pulsing and trying to work with the fading frenzy he had produced in me.

This man. I didn't have words for how he made me feel. I wanted to say it felt like a glorious death when I succumbed to him, but that wasn't really right. I had never wanted to die, and especially not now. All the things I had ever wished for as a girl, the things I could never put a name to, were right here between us. The yearning, the striving, the need for a connection with something outside myself so deep that I lost track of where my own mind ended and the universe began. He was leading me down a path to all of that. When he could finally touch me, I knew it would be even farther out of the reach of words.

"Gretel," he said. "I've been waiting all my life for something I didn't understand. It was you." He looked like he wanted to kiss me so badly that I actually drew back, on the verge of telling him to be careful. He stopped and bowed to me instead. Then he set me free. "Now, we have a lot of sweets to make and not much time."

# Chapter Ten

GRETEL

I HAD no time to decorate the desserts. I made little cups of raspberries and cream while he set to baking two cakes. We managed to fill the counter before a courier came to take the bounty to the revels, but just barely.

That night, we shared the same bed, a roll of blankets between us, and I slept so well near his warmth. Growing up in a cottage with only one common room and a single bedroom, I was used to hearing someone else breathe near me. If he teased me in the middle of the night, I didn't even remember it. But I did yearn for him, always. I wanted to yearn for him always. As days went by I started thinking more and more what a relief it was that he never questioned my own desires. He never shamed me for having them, never treated me like I was some aberrant creature sprung out of the farm like a two-headed calf. My desires were his, and his desires were mine, and both of our desires were insatiable and unending.

I had never imagined I'd be so happy.

And the work certainly didn't hurt. More days passed, and I felt that at some point, we would run out of recipes. We never did. We turned out small cups of mousse, light yet rich; glazed dried plums that tasted almost alcoholic, stuffed with vanilla cream; cheesecakes covered in tiny leaves of chocolate in the shape of a tree, just like my dress; hard candies flavored with the juice of tiny, almost floral tasting limes and dusted in fine sugar. Growing up in poverty on a farm, do you suppose I had ever even tasted a lime before? Never!

"They come in fresh in the port cities," the Magus said. "Hansel may have tasted them. Their price is not too dear in Hausach."

I bristled at the thought of Hansel. Which was funny, because I missed him all the time. His presence was always in the edges of my mind. It was mixed with shame, though. I was happy, but he could never ever see me like this, I thought. He would not see happiness. He would see me like the whores on the church ceiling who had to be blessed by St. Yktrin.

"You haven't written your brother," the Magus said.

"No...I don't like lying."

"Even if you must lie, I think you should write. You want him to worry? He'll come after you if he doesn't hear something. Just make up a story about working for Anna. I know you're clever enough for that."

That was true. I supposed I had to say something. "I can't lie to my brother. He knows me too well."

"You can't tell him the truth. He's made up his mind. He'll come here and make trouble."

That evening before I came to bed I tried to write a letter. Hansel would expect more than a few lines. He would want details of my new life, from the work to the weather to the people I was meeting. I should invent a fictional life, but I couldn't seem to think of anything except the moment at hand. My life with the Magus had a bracing immediacy. That was partly what I loved about it. I was no longer dreaming of something that would never happen. Each moment, I felt fully in my skin.

If I lied to him, I would lose him. And losing my twin, my only family? That was not an option.

*Curse it all.*

The quill scratched furiously along the paper.

*Dear Hansel,*

*I must be honest with you although I know you might never understand. I have gone to live with the Magus. He is under a curse. If we break the curse, we can be properly married. Until then, he is unable to touch me, and I tell you, he has not corrupted me in any way that I was not already corrupted long ago by my own thoughts. Go ahead and clutch your heart in horror.*

*I don't know why, but I was born a creature of passions, Hansel. But when I think about it, we weren't that different. You love Peter and society says you should not. If you could make life easier on yourself and ignore that love you feel, would you? I don't think you would give that up. And it doesn't matter, does it? It's not possible. I feel the same way.*

*You said I never judged you for loving Peter. I never will. But you would judge me for what I feel. It hurts me when I think about it, because I love you and I would rather be honest. I struggle to write you now, because I know you won't approve, but I don't want you to worry that something has happened to me. I actually tried to lie and say I was working for Anna, but I simply can't.*

*YOUR LOVING SISTER ALWAYS,*
   *Gretel*

IN THE MORNING, the Magus said, "I think you could use some sunshine. You spend too much time shut up in here. Why don't you journey to Pillna and take the letter to town to mail?"

"Alone?" I had never left my village without Hansel. No woman walked beyond the gates without a chaperone to protect her.

"I'll give you a charm. It'll ward off the bears in the woods. You'll be all right in the village. Go to Anna if anyone gives you trouble. Hold still." He took a necklace from his pocket. His golden eyes regarded me fondly as he fastened the clasp at the back of my neck, careful not to touch my skin. "Someone must go. I need to stay here and make the desserts. You can change back into your old clothing for this."

I touched the green stone that now hung just below the blue one he had given me before. He was letting me walk through the woods and go to a town where I barely knew anyone. "You trust me?"

He lifted a brow. "Shouldn't I?"

"It's strange to have freedom... Every moment I've been here has belonged to you."

"I'm not worried you'll forget me," he said. "But it would be quite ridiculous if you never left the house. There are parts of you I wish to fully possess. But your feet are not among them. A walk will do you good."

The freedom to walk out the door and travel on my own was not something I had even realized I could have, but now that I could, I wanted it badly. I set off down the path and for the first time, I could savor the beauty of the woods while setting my own pace, and it was wonderful. Better yet, the Magus told me I could buy a new dress and new embroidery thread. My old dress no longer fit. I was well fed for the first time in my life and my curves had filled in. The bodice laces were strained wide, and I had to cut the waist of the skirt, covering the gap with an apron.

I reached town in the afternoon and went straight to the dry goods shop, eager to select my colors of thread. Another woman was already keeping the shopkeeper occupied, looking at bolts of fabric.

"Give me a good thick wool," she said. "Olvar wants a winter coat and I need to make something for little Roland, come winter. How about that green one?" She pointed at a bolt on the top shelf. As the wiry old shopkeeper climbed a ladder on knees that seemed somewhat arthritic, the woman sighed and looked at me with a slightly apologetic smile.

Then her eyes glanced over the necklace with the charm, to my face, and then my clothes. She didn't say anything, but she lingered and browsed after her cloth had been cut, and I was nervous picking out the thread. I had so been looking forward to this and now a stranger was shadowing me. When I left the shop with my dress and thread in a box, she followed me out.

"Miss?"

I turned, trying not to betray any nerves. "I don't know why you're following me."

"I think that's a faery necklace. Where did you get it?"

"Oh—I bought it in a marketplace somewhere. Please, I have business to attend to before dark."

"Have you been to the Wicked Revels?"

"No."

"You have that...look," she said. "You don't live here in town, do you?"

I pushed through the door of the inn. Anna was at the counter with the tourist trinkets today. "Oh," she said. "Gretel...and Jeannie. You two don't...know each other, do you?"

"No," I said. "I just need to send a letter."

Jeannie followed me to the counter.

I put my hands on my hips. "I don't know who you are or what you want with me, but it's rude."

She chuckled. "I am known to be rude when I want information."

"There's no information to be had with me."

"You're with *him*, aren't you? The last king."

"I—I don't know what you're talking about."

"Don't worry, I'm not going to tell anyone if you're not in trouble or trying to make trouble," Jeannie said. "Will can be hot headed. Then again, so can I. I suppose I gave him the knife that killed the king, but I didn't think he'd actually kill anyone, you know."

"Killed...the Magus," I said. This was what the Trickster Mage was talking about. "How did it happen?"

"Simple enough, really. Will put my knife into his back. Not very honorable, but it wasn't a fair fight either; the faery king had magic and Will didn't."

"Are you...the Queen of the Wicked Revels?"

She laughed. "No, no, spare me from being queen of anything! I'm Will's sister. Lately, I've been the nursemaid of the Wicked Revels, keeping an eye on young Prince Roland and the baby. How's that for a romantic position? I married a wood elf who isn't much for dancing. We're happier playing cards by the fire. I'm no threat, really, but you can't blame me for wondering what the last king is up to. I love my brother dearly."

"I understand," I said, feeling a pang.

"After the king died," Jeannie continued, "his people took him to bury. And one would normally expect that was the end of it. But it wasn't. He came back. A bit paler, a bit more drawn, but alive as anyone. Now, I'm told it happens, and far be it from me to judge, but I expect he made a bargain with someone quite wicked."

"The Trickster Mage..."

"I don't know him," Jeannie said. "But *he* sounds like a man best avoided."

"The Trickster Mage said..." I tried to form the words. *The Magus will die on Samhain night if he can't touch me.* But my throat strained and nothing came out.

"What's wrong, love?" Jeannie asked. I was starting to like the woman, although I resisted it with all my being.

"I—I can't say. But the Magus needs help. He's not a bad man."

"His sentence will be lifted in just a few weeks," Jeannie said. "Or are you wanting to come to the Revels with him? Well, I hardly think that's a good idea. The Magus and Will are about as fond of each other as a house cat and a barn cat."

"Why, exactly, did your brother kill him?" I asked, my tone careful.

Jeannie shifted her packages in her arms. "You know what? Let's have a seat and talk over a bit of ale. My treat. Anna?" She caught the attention of the proprietress and pointed at a table. Before I knew it, I was in deeper than before, our parcels stacked up together in an empty chair, and both of us sitting together by the window. I'm sure this was not what the Magus had in mind when he sent me to town alone, but I wanted to hear the other side of the story.

"He was trying to protect Princess Evaline," Jeannie

said. "The old king lured the Princess Evaline, trying to get her mask from her. When Eva gave her mask to Will, your Magus said they both belonged to him, in the end. He tied her up in his bond tree. And they fought over her and did what men do. Will thought the king was a wicked faery, and perhaps he wasn't wrong. A lot of the Revelers themselves wanted the king gone. But perhaps the old king also thought he had a right to her. Faeries don't always play by the same rules as humans."

"I don't know...what went on between them." I flushed. "He said the power of the masks corrupted him. But the Magus—I feel sure he doesn't want to hurt anyone. He just wants to live his life. He doesn't deserve this sentence, not to be able to touch anyone..."

"It isn't forever. His time is almost up! Will's sentence didn't seem too harsh to me. He just doesn't want the old king playing his old tricks. You must see, from my brother's perspective, that the Magus, as you call him, tried to trap both of them in the Wicked Revels, feeding their sexual power to him, through the tree. The other faeries asked Will to be rid of him. And then, after he was killed, he came back from the dead! No wise ruler would give too much leeway to a man like that. My brother must protect his kingdom. One doesn't just let one's rivals waltz through the gates."

"We just want to be free to marry..." Only, this wasn't true, from the Magus' perspective. He was planning to take back the throne. I hated the thought. If the Magus could have me, maybe he would give up on the rest.

"His sentence is up on All Saints' Day, just after All Hallow's Eve," she said. "And then you can marry him. Just hold on for a few weeks!"

"Oh Jeannie, you've been so kind. I beg you, couldn't Will end the sentence just a little early?"

Jeannie's brows furrowed. "You know I can't ask him to do that. Perhaps if the Magus swore his allegiance to Will, that would be one thing. But without something in return, a king can't go soft on a punishment that was already generous enough."

Damn it all. It was so simple, but the Magus would die for the sake of his pride. "Just a *day* early?"

Jeannie sighed gently. "I don't know what bargain he made with this Trickster Mage, but if the Magus won't make any concessions, then you'll have to contend with his terms. A cruel king could have killed or maimed or imprisoned the old king. I think my brother has been quite fair. "

# Chapter Eleven

✧❦✧

GRETEL

"GRETEL, I am aware of how unfortunate this situation is," the Magus said when I returned home. I was honest with him about my meeting with Jeannie. Time was running out for us. "You think I haven't gone over every angle of it?"

"Are you sure...if you tried to make peace with the current King and Queen...," I ventured. "Have you ever apologized?"

He said, in a slightly halting way, "Yes...for my mistakes, of course."

"I can tell this wasn't a very good apology."

"Do you want me to *grovel* and *beg*, Gretel? I am a *king*!"

"You're a baker," I said softly, although it made him snarl. "And you're wonderful at it. We make such beautiful things together. Do you want to be king again because you would truly rather be king? Or because you just don't want to serve someone else? I *love*—this—" I waved at the kitchen. "And I love you. And I don't know if I really want to be the queen. Not if it means we can't make things together anymore."

He took a deep breath, his nostrils flaring slightly, his anger restrained. I thought he was going to order me to get on the rack and despite that I was really very upset at him, the thought still aroused me.

Instead, he said, "Let's take a ride."

"A ride? On what? You don't have any horses."

"I don't keep them in a stable, but who says I don't have horses? Perhaps we both need fresh air today. Did you get a new dress in Pillna, Gretel?"

His voice made me shiver when it took on that slight tone of command. I thought this might not be an ordinary ride, but part of the game. "Yes."

"Let me see."

I opened the box and took out the dress. Like all of the dresses of the region, it had a sleeveless bodice that dipped into a V in the back to show off a bit of lace blouse, and had a low neckline in front, just below the nipples, supporting the breasts. Young maidens wore the blouse beneath the dress fairly low to show off the mounds of their breasts, while older women wore blouses with a higher neck. The bodice laced in front and the skirt fell several inches above the feet to display the ankles and neatly laced boots.

"I chose the simplest black wool this time," I said. "To show the colors of the embroidery. I might have gone a little wild with buying the thread."

"Spent all the coin I gave you, hm?"

"I'm afraid so. But you did give it to me."

He ran the wool between his fingers. "Very soft. Not too itchy. You'll be glad of that. Take off *all* of your clothes including undergarments and put this on instead."

I pulled off my dress and laid it on the table. Despite this distraction, I had not forgotten our argument. I looked at the pastry dough in progress and the bowl of berries and I wondered briefly, *Does he hate this work? Is our happiness more on my end than his, because he is dreaming of taking back the throne? I don't believe it. He gets lost in this. I've seen it in his eyes. Taking back the throne has nothing to do with happiness, only with pride.*

I stripped down bare except for the necklaces.

"You can give me back the charm," he said. "We won't encounter any bears or wolves while we're riding. Just wear the choker. You have the most exquisite neck."

I took off the charm and handed it back to him. He picked up his wand and stroked the tip back and forth across my wet sex just long enough to quicken my breath, then sucked the tip clean. "Put on your new dress," he said.

I dropped it over my head and slid my arms through, pulling the bodice down over me. The fabric was soft, but nevertheless it scratched my nipples as it brushed by.

He took the ribbons of the bodice in his own hands. I stood still as he tightened them, one by one, with an air of such careful concentration. The Magus was a man who could pour such a singular focus into the smallest moment, whether it was tightening a lace or squeezing the perfect dollop of cream into the hollow of a pastry. I had a wave of unbearable anticipation, thinking of the day when he could touch me, when all the careful intensity of his hands and eyes was trained on me alone, with nothing in the way.

As the bodice tightened, my breasts were pushed up higher into soft, round mounds with my nipples hard and pointed. He tied the lace in a little bow at my waist.

"You can put your boots on now," he said. "And then, come with me."

I pulled on my stockings and laced up my boots, and we walked outside. He whistled several long, wispy notes.

"It takes a little time," he said, as we stood there together under the cover of the forest. "We'll only be able to take a short ride, and maybe a short ride is all you can manage anyway."

"I haven't had much experience riding," I said, a little confused as to why he didn't think I could manage the ride. "We never had money for horses. We had to borrow them from the neighbors for things Hansel simply couldn't do himself."

"It doesn't matter, with these horses," he said. "They are smarter than human horses, and very attuned to you. They won't spook or ride faster than you can manage or go off in the wrong direction. If you can keep your feet in the stirrups, you'll be fine."

I felt their hoofbeats pound the ground a second before I heard them, and several long seconds passed before we saw them charging down the path, two beautiful white horses that seemed larger than I expected.

"Maybe you should take off your apron," I said. "Even though it's cute on you, you will look so elegant all in black on a white horse."

"Cute on me?" he said, distastefully.

"You don't like being cute?" I asked, delighted to have found a way to tease him. "Too bad."

He frowned and tugged the knot free behind him, hanging the apron on the nearest tree branch. "Wait a moment while I saddle them."

While he walked off toward a shed standing a little ways away from the house, one of the horses came up to me and lowered its head like it wanted to be petted, with the other one following a step behind. Horses usually made me a little nervous because back in Aupenburg, the men always dealt with them, and I could count on one hand the number of ladies who rode their own horses. But these seemed like another species. They approached me slowly and calmly like they identified my anxiety and didn't want to frighten me. I ran my hands along their noses and manes.

"You're softer than I expected," I said. "Soft, faery horses..."

The Magus came back with saddles and got our mounts ready for us while he told me to bring them some apples from the house.

"How will I get up into the saddle?" I asked. "They're so tall and you can't lift me up."

"I can touch your waist through the dress for a moment or two before it burns me," he said. "We'll hurry."

He put his hands on me and practically tossed me up onto the horse like a hot potato as I managed to fling my leg over and grab the saddle awkwardly. The horse was very patient with our clumsiness; she didn't move a hair except to glance back as if to check on me.

But once I was up there settling into the saddle I realized that my saddle was specially made. It held me firmly in place with just a little wiggle room, supporting the curve of my buttocks and pelvis, and was made out of very soft leather that was comfortable against my naked skin— except where my clit rested. Here, there was a panel of soft pointed bumps that were formed precisely to tease me with every movement of my horse. I don't know how on earth they were made. When I tried to adjust away from them they only seemed to worm their way deeper into my folds. I could lift myself off the saddle but that was hard to maintain for more than a few seconds.

While I considered this new development, the Magus had gotten onto his horse and rode up alongside me with the most devilish grin. "You didn't think I would suggest an ordinary afternoon, did you? You thought I'd give you a break? I have to keep surprising you to keep the magic potent. Especially when you've been such a defiant girl, speaking with great sympathy to the family who usurped me..."

Strangely, I had a feeling I had actually made him think. If he was truly upset, he wouldn't be grinning at me and making conversation about it while I was so vulnerable. I lifted my chin high and cast my eyes away from him. "It isn't so much that I sympathize with people I barely know, as that I think you're making a mistake. I don't think we will ever be happier doing something else as we are right now, you and I, making magical things together."

He gave my horse a little smack on the rump and she started cantering down the path.

I could only shudder forward and clutch at her mane. Every movement of the horse rippled up into my tender sex and sent an absolutely agonizing pleasure through my spread legs until my toes were clenching in my boots. I hated him and I loved him for doing these things to me. He drove me out of my mind.

He rode up beside me and made a low whistle that seemed to signal my horse to slow back down into more of a trot, which I'm not sure was any better for me.

"Sit up straight," he said. I forced my spine upward. I wanted to double over. I wanted to clutch the neck of this horse and claw its skin. Shudders of pleasure kept passing over me and my hands were shaking.

He admired my pert bare breasts, briefly tracing the outline of them with his wand. Feeling his eyes on me made it all the worse. "Please...please, Magus..." I gasped, burning with heat, trying to wriggle away from the constant little brushing sensations stimulating me at multiple angles.

"Are you going to come, Gretel?"

"I—" I choked out a sob. "I need to."

"But do you think you will?"

"No..." Like everything else he did to me, it was not quite enough. I hunched over again, sobbing with torture as the teasing sensation just continued on and on and there was nowhere I could go unless I flung myself off a moving horse. "Please, Magus...*please!*"

He drew close enough to me that our boots bumped against each other, and he tapped my chin with the tip of the wand. "Can you bear it, Gretel?"

I swallowed back a lump in my throat, tamping down the sharpest edges of what I felt. I knew what I had to say. "Yes..."

"It gets more difficult," he said, "as the time draws closer. That is to be expected. We will ride again before Samhain."

"If it turns out that you have to die on Samhain night," I said, "I want to bloody kill you myself."

He laughed and spurred his horse ahead of me.

# Chapter Twelve

GRETEL

WHEN WE GOT BACK, he started boiling water. "You did very well today, my sweet Gretel. I know these final days will test you, most especially."

"It's worth enduring...if I get you at the end of it. But I want you. Not the King of the Revels. Just you."

He rapped his fingers on the table. I knew by now that this gesture meant I was saying something he didn't want to hear. "The King of the Wicked Revels and me...they were one and the same for fifteen years, Gretel." He paused. "I'll finish the work today. Take a nice warm bath."

I had never known it before, but there was a little room off of the kitchen with a clawfoot tub. I could have sworn that door led to the backyard. I soaked there and he made me a cup of hot chocolate and brought more hot water now and then, so despite the chilly autumn air, it stayed comfortable. My nerves wound down and I started to relax so deeply I almost nodded off in the tub.

I had never felt so wonderfully spent, if not quite satisfied. No matter what he did to me, even if it was torturous at the time, in hindsight I wanted more of it. The idea that we would ride again brought a sense of dread, and the idea that we might never ride again was far, far worse.

Indeed, every two or three or four days (he never told me when it would happen, just to keep me in suspense) we would take a break and he would summon the horses. We rode until I could do nothing but beg him to touch me. Every day, I lasted a little longer and at the end of it I always had a hot bath and chocolate. In the evening I started working on embroidering my dress with two white horses on the back of the skirt.

I was counting the days until Samhain, the day when we would sneak into the Wicked Revels.

Aramy came one afternoon when I was in the bath. The Magus shut the door on me. "Stay here," he said.

I recognized Aramy's voice from my first night in the Magus' house. I heard them whispering. I crept quietly out of the tub, bundling myself in a towel but still shivering, and pressed my ear to the door.

"Everything is set," I heard Aramy say. "On Samhain night, they will all wear masks. No one will notice you in the crowd. Your nephew is already on the march and he's supported by the Swift River faery clan." Softer murmuring between them. It was quite nefarious to murmur, I thought.

"Yes," Aramy said then, more emphatically. "The people want you. Your plan has worked beautifully. I never thought you'd find a girl who was willing to go through with it all. I can't imagine how she must feel. Every bite of those cakes and chocolates is infused with such delicate yearning and temptation. You should see their faces when they eat them. They want more of what you can give them."

The Magus hesitated. "I know this magic," he said. "I understand my people. A man like Will—"

"Could never truly manage the Wicked Revels," Aramy said. "Never doubt that you are the true king, my lord. The humans will leave if we have to put their heads on spears!"

My chest clenched.

"Hush," the Magus whispered sharply. "It won't come to that."

"It would serve them—"

"Hush!" the Magus was fierce now. "Mind your place. I told you it won't come to that."

"Will murdered you."

"I might have done the same, in Will's shoes."

"My lord—" Aramy laughed uncomfortably. "I didn't make a deal with the Trickster Mage just to go soft on the people who killed you."

"I am sure, deep down, the humans might be relieved to return to their own lands. They will leave in peace. I know it. We are not tyrants. They will leave with their heads intact and their hearts still beating."

"Of course. I serve you, my lord..."

They moved toward the front door and I couldn't hear them anymore. I heard the door shut but several more long moments passed before the Magus opened my door. I was back in the tub now, but it was getting cold and I was too anxious to enjoy it.

He tested the water temperature with his finger, and sighed. "I apologize. I'll heat up more water."

"I know Aramy saved your life, but I hope you can really trust him," I said.

"Snooping at doors, are we?"

"You can't blame me."

"He talks big, but there is no need for a violent coup. That's why I've taken the time to win favor with my desserts. And although Aramy's had to organize the operation, I will be leading the charge when the time comes. They will all listen to me."

"I hope so," I said, grabbing the towel. "No need to heat up more water. I've turned into a prune while you were talking. Anyway, I'd rather work in the bake shop while I still *can*." He hadn't said anything to Aramy about wanting to stay a baker with me, and so I knew I hadn't changed his mind.

I dried off and went to fetch my clothes.

"No, don't dress," he said. "Go to the rack."

"You need my help to finish the icings," I said.

"I managed without you for a long time."

"You're punishing me?" I picked up my clothes anyway. "Why? Because I told you not to trust Aramy? Because I like running a bake shop with you?"

"You don't love the real me," he said. "The King of the Wicked Revels is the real me. You love whatever this is. It's time you moved past it."

My mouth snapped open in annoyance before I said, "I don't know 'the King of the Wicked Revels'. I love this *and* you, because it's wonderful. We're wonderful together, and I just can't believe that you don't see it. Oh no, I think you do see it. You *know* that you're a better baker than you were a king."

He flinched.

I seized on this moment of weakness. "You're just being proud. You can't stand that someone else took your place, but in the end, what does it matter? You messed up the Revels; you said so yourself."

"Hush, girl!" he barked at me, and the wand he usually

flicked so delicately was now picked up from the table and swung with as much vigor as Hansel cutting down the wheat. Some unseen force of magic shoved my body backward and the arms of the rack swung down to catch me in bonds. I felt almost like a person was snatching me up from behind and plucking my feet right off the ground as the wood snapped around my ankles. I shrieked, disoriented.

Then I struggled. For once, this wasn't what I wanted and he knew it. He was glaring down at the table.

"Let me *go*," I said.

He rapped the table with his fingers. Then he looked up at me slowly.

"This conversation isn't part of our game," I said.

He seemed to drift far away even as he looked at me, and then he walked up to me. I locked on his eyes, still struggling, getting more annoyed the longer he kept being so silent and moving so slowly. It was seductive when I wanted to be seduced. It was irritating when I wanted to discuss our future.

He half-smiled. "You're not afraid to defy me even a little, are you?"

"Maybe a little. You did just fling me backward and trap me and you have a history of surprising me. But I'm not letting it stop me." I lifted my chin. "I have this feeling no one's given you any outside perspective on your life in a long time. Well, you gave me some perspective on mine. So it's only fair."

He reached for a wisp of hair that would never stay in my braid, but always popped out above my ear, and pulled it gently between his fingers. I felt his touch through that little strand of hair. Even this made him snap his fingers back and rub them. My hair left pink lines on his skin. "In Ellurine," he said, "the queen submits to the king in all things. That is her role on the stage of my homeland. I used to watch my mother play it perfectly. And I told myself, never. I *never* wanted that. And yet, it is so easy to become the thing we never wanted to be. It sneaks up on us when we're not looking."

"But it's not too late to change back," I said.

He tapped my bonds and I stepped down.

"I apologize, my Gretel...I could use help with the icing, after all. I can't decorate the cakes half as well."

I slipped on my dress and picked up a bowl and we said no more about it. But he still hadn't addressed the real issue at hand.

*Maybe it won't be so bad to be a queen,* I thought. *I can still embroider and make cakes in my idle hours if I wish, can't I?* But if he wasn't there at my side, it wasn't the same. Maybe I was the one wishing for too much. Hansel said I always wanted my potential husband to be perfect. I suppose the Magus was perfect in every other way, and soon he would be able to touch me, and maybe I would forget all about the time we spent in this kitchen, after all.

I watched him juggling a pan of toasted nuts and then a pot of melting chocolate and finally a bowl of whipping cream in short order, and I knew—I would miss this forever.

# Chapter Thirteen

✤

## THE MAGUS

THAT NIGHT, I put a little sleeping draught in Gretel's wine. While she was sleeping, I slipped out of bed. I paused to admire her peaceful face, her cheeks pink and rosy from good food and sunshine. Her long golden hair was bound in a loose braid that fell across the layers of blankets that kept her safe and warm. She had changed so much since she first came to me. Every day, she looked healthier and more confident.

Before Gretel, I only knew the human girls that I lured to my fleeting dance. I seduced them in the dizzying chaos of the Revels.

I had never known this. A domestic life: calm, quiet, companionable. I had never been so attuned to the girls I danced with and held in my arms, as I was to this girl whom I could never touch. She always seemed to know what I needed.

*Except this.*

She wanted me to stay here, in this house that wasn't my own, in this life that wasn't my own. She wanted me to let Will remain king. I was downright offended when I pondered it, that she would consider this life worthy of me. That she had even suggested I should apologize to him. I might have made mistakes, but this was my world, not Will's. I deserved to take it back.

*She has no idea,* I thought.

I had never seen the Wicked Revels under the rule of these humans. Tonight, I decided, with Samhain mere nights away, I would take the risk of scouting the situation.

Clad and cloaked in plain black garments, so different from the beautiful clothes I had worn as king, I summoned one of the horses and rode down the path I had not taken in three years. My eyes adjusted quickly to the darkness. I missed all of this; the brisk smoke-scented air of an autumn night and the moon high and bright in a clear sky. My pulse quickened as I drew closer. I assumed I would reach the Revels at the back of the forest, the king's entrance, but instead I came upon the Three Precious Groves, the gateway to our realm where humans would normally enter, with leaves of silver, gold, and diamonds. I left my horse behind and continued on foot, skirting around the groves so I wouldn't run into the handmaidens.

The Revels were across the river. I could see the glow of lights, hear the music.

From this perspective, they seemed like a theater, and I had been transformed from player to audience, no longer allowed backstage. Paths had always been tricky in this world, and the path had changed for me. I had to cross the river now, whereas once my path led me right to the dance. I should have known.

I stripped off my clothes and bundled them, holding them on the top of my head so they would stay dry. It was a shallow enough river that I could keep my feet on the ground, but the currents were fast in places. I was breathing hard by the time I battled my way across, but I brushed off my exhaustion, drew my clothes back on, and forged onward.

The music was louder now. I turned toward the forest rather than entering the Revels directly. I wanted simply to observe, not to be seen. I knew these woods as well as anyone in all the world, including every little spot for a rendezvous. It was easy for me to avoid the clearing where I heard a couple whispering to each other, and the tree where a man pinned a laughing faery lady against the bark. I made my way up to the highest point, where a gentle hill swelled up behind the musicians, and crouched beneath the brush.

From here, I could see the entire dance laid out before me. The first thing I noticed were the long tables of food. The food was similar to what Gretel and I ate every day, but with much more variety. The Wicked Revels had several chefs. Vegetables, bread and meat were in abundance. Pears were stacked in towers. A roasted goose still had one half of its breast uncarved. The food was meant to last all night.

The sweets were completely wiped out already. Some of the trays were even on the ground like the table had been violently ransacked. Yes, my magic was working on the people. They snapped up every last bit of sugar and spice, chocolate and cream. I could not help a surge of pride in that. I had been working alone, never getting to see for myself how my labors were appreciated.

The dance was as frenzied and wild as ever. When I was the king, I never came up to the hill to watch. From this vantage point it was a kaleidoscope of twirling couples and swirling skirts and cloaks.

The vision blurred for a moment and I saw the court of my homeland, like a faraway dream. My father and mother, aunts and uncles and distant cousins, all dressed in elaborate clothing, hair towered high into sculptures and hats sporting plumes and gold ornaments. Every step of the dance was prescribed. It was bad etiquette if one lady's skirt brushed another. My father was the king, the shining sun. My mother was beside him. She was never permitted to wear the dress of Ellurine, but wore the foreign robes of the Queen Who Bowed, as all queens had since the first. My mother was certainly not the only one whose character was set for her. My uncle was given the role of the faithful servant to the crown, honored with the symbol of the stag, while my father's cousin the Duchess of Arshain was the leading courtesan who didn't have to pledge herself to a single man and wore the symbol of the many-colored bird. Each role was marked by its own costumes, colors, sigils and mannerisms. The other children and I used to watch them from a high balcony, forbidden from the evening balls until we were initiated into the dance.

The Revels was the opposite of those balls of my memories. From the first moment I saw this dance, it was all I had ever wanted.

In the Revels, you could be anyone you wanted to be. You could dance how you liked, and dress how you liked. You could be shy one day and bold the next.

The music was loud, the drums pounding with the vigor of an impending battle while the fiddles danced with the joy of a holiday. Two fiddles now? There hadn't been two fiddlers when I was the king. Will had added a few musicians.

I had to admit, the music was good. Were the dancers as numerous? Did they have the same abandon and wild lust as they did before? They seemed to wear more clothes than they did before. Not a bare breast in sight. I scoffed. Modesty rules would be very human indeed. And it was strange to see the girls without masks. I knew that policy had to end, but it had added some mystery.

Will was sitting on the royal dais in the throne that had once been mine. He stretched his bad leg and I narrowed my eyes. *He probably doesn't dance much. What a shame for the King of the Revels to be a cripple.*

*Look at him there, just watching. Probably thinking of what else of mine he can change.*

I sought the queen next. She was dancing with their firstborn, a boy who was an eternal baby in my mind but was now doing a clumsy jig with his small hands caught in his mother's. Children at the Revels? I looked around. I saw a few babes but none older. At least there didn't seem to be any children old enough to understand.

*Still.*

As one song ended, Will called out something, and everyone cheered. Queen Evaline shouted to him and the crowd laughed. The band kicked in with a new rhythm and Will sang in a voice as clear and perfect as any singer I'd ever engaged.


*I WENT to war a country boy and to my love I said goodbye*
*I came back brave as any man but missing me an eye*
*Yes, missing me an eye*


*I WENT to war a strapping lad fat on pork and eggs*
*I came back lean and sharp and strong but missing me a leg*
*Yes, missing me a leg*

*SHE SAID she'd love me evermore, dropped kisses on my scars*
  *My lady pledged her love to me beneath the moon and stars*


*I WENT to war a hearty gent and said goodbye to Brigit*
  *Came back the hero of my realm but missing me a digit*
  *Yes, missing me a digit*


*SHE LOOKED ME UP, she looked me down, she asked me what I*
*meant*
  *I said th' shrapnel got the most of it and what is left is bent*
  *Yes, what is left is bent*


*MY LOVE she backed away from me with tears across her face*
  *If I can't fuck you now, she said, someone else can take your*
*place*


THE REVELERS WERE CLAPPING and laughing heartily at this bawdy humor while Queen Evaline jumped up beside her husband, kissed his cheek, said, "In no way an accurate reflection, mind you!" to more laughter, and they danced a bit despite Will's stiff leg to the instrumental break, the fiddles each taking a turn at ever faster reels.

*Humor?* I picked up a pinecone and pitched it into the crowd before I hurried back down the slope. The Revels weren't supposed to be *funny*. Leave it to a human to make a mockery of the whole thing, and what traitors they were to laugh!

I heard him singing a ballad now in the distance, his voice undeniably pure. No matter how much I hated Will,

I could not deny his talent. I could deny the merriment of the dance, the singing of those twin fiddles.

As I crossed the river again, I realized how reckless I had been tonight. If I had been caught, I might have blown the whole plan to ambush the Samhain festivities and Gretel would be found out and sent away.

I stormed home, my mind racing over what I had seen. Impostors taking over my Revels, changing everything without any regard for ritual. Humans. Humans who seemed stupidly in love, bringing their children to the dance. I had once held the Princess Evaline in my arms. She had almost been mine.

*What am I thinking? Jealous of Will for marrying Evaline? I never loved her.*

As I crossed the threshold, my temper rushed out of me. Everything here reminded me of my Gretel. Even when she was safe and sound, sleeping in her bed, I could feel her presence. I could see her moving from room to room, imagine her intense little face when she was working and her pleading eyes when I teased her.

I climbed the stairs. Gretel slept in the moonlight, so exquisite that I could hardly breathe. Her hand was draped across the pillow and her fingers twitched like she was working on something, even in her dreams.

I would never have been happy like this with Evaline. She was too timid. Too placid. Too much a princess.

Gretel was always the one.

It struck me not just how much I wanted to make her happy, but how happy we already were.

When I thought of Will sitting on my throne, I wanted to strike him.

Those were my people who had been laughing along with him, as boisterous as ever. Some of them had turned against me to put Will on the throne in the first place. I had always struggled to believe it, but now I saw with my own eyes how the new king was accepted, whether I liked it or not. He looked strong while I was weak and forgotten. I would be dead right now if not for Aramy. He had brought me back to reclaim my throne, not to bake cakes, but I wondered what would happen when we ambushed the Revels.

I cursed softly.

Maybe Gretel was right. I wasn't taking back the Revels to make us happy. I was doing it out of pride, just to prove that I could.

Gretel rolled onto her back, giving me a dreamy smile. "Mmm...why are you awake?"

"I went to the Revels tonight."

She sat up. "Why?"

"No one saw me. I went to think."

"And did you think?"

"Yes."

Her brow furrowed. "It sounds like you were up to some mischief. I thought you were forbidden from going there?"

"I didn't really...enter the Revels. I just watched from afar. Facing some of the darker places of my soul." I unbuttoned my shirt.

She lifted her hand to brush the fabric of my shirt, lightly, with her fingertips. She seemed only half aware of the waking world, and I cringed back, afraid she would burn my skin. But her hand dropped. "This is where you belong," she said. "Here with me."

"I wish it were that simple."

"It is that simple," she whispered. "You're the one who's too complicated."

I ran my hand through my hair. Her words came as if from a dream. And who had ever known me as well as this girl? Who had looked into my eyes again and again as we shared our deepest desire with each other? I even talked to her about Ellurine, and I never talked of home to anyone. I had a dread of becoming of my father, of having a wife like my mother.

I didn't want to be lord and master of my realm like Father was. I didn't want a wife who submitted to me in all things. Gretel saw me better than I saw myself, and she told me so.

She yawned. "I'm very tired, Magus."

"I gave you a bit of sleeping draught tonight. I knew that otherwise you'd feel me leaving the bed. I needed to do this alone."

"And what did you do? What did you see?" she asked. "Is it as bad as you thought?"

I couldn't quite bring myself to say the words. *My people are happy with Will. And I am happy here with you.* It was true, perhaps, but it was also poison on my tongue. *King Will.*

I shook my head. It was too late to back out on my plan with Aramy. He had made a deal with the Trickster Mage, gathered my nephew and other faery clans to aid me in my claim to the throne. It would be selfish of me to change my mind. Even Marte didn't want a human to be king. The Revels had been the domain of faeries as long as anyone could remember.

"No matter what we become," I told her, "we won't forget our time here. We will continue to make things together. Beautiful things."

She let out the smallest sigh. I knew she was hoping for something else. I wished I could make her understand how things had to be. I couldn't just surrender to the man who had driven a knife into me.

I peeled back the covers and settled beside her, but

sleep would not come. I watched her for a little while, and imagined what might happen if Will and his family were killed because of me. It would be the end of his song, the end of his young child, and my people would take sides even more than they already did.

ARAMY CAME by just before Samhain. "All is in place," he said. "The Revelers will enter the human world after sunset to play their tricks on the human townsfolk, as they always do, and when they are vulnerable, we'll strike."

On the night of Samhain, the veil between the human world and the Revels vanished. It was a long held tradition for the Revelers to venture out and pound on the doors of the local humans. If the humans offered food to the faeries, the Revelers gave them a blessing. If they were ignored, they would receive a small curse, hex, or act of petty vandalism. No one was ever hurt, but legend suggested that if we didn't menace the humans, they would enter our world instead.

"I am sure Will and Evaline have no idea what's about to befall them," Aramy said. "They'll be weakened away from the forest. We'll scatter them and force Will and Evaline to give the Revels back to you. They can stay in the human world, and we can go home."

"Whatever happens, they must leave safely. An assassination is not possible."

"Yes, yes, you told me last time," Aramy said. "You are certainly concerned for their welfare, aren't you? It's that girl, isn't it? She's encouraging you to be gentle to fellow humans."

"You may have saved my life, but you still have no right to speak to me that way. All my life, I have wanted nothing more than to be King of the Revels. But last night, I snuck in to the forest and saw the people dancing to Will's song. Trust me, if we kill that man, it will be far worse for us."

"He killed *you*."

"I am well aware. But I was under the addictive influence of magic and not quite myself. Perhaps I deserved it. Don't get me wrong, Aramy. I want the throne back, but if you disobey my command, my first act as king will be holding your trial."

Aramy flushed with anger he couldn't hide, but he held onto his composure and quickly bowed. "As you say, my lord. You know more about these matters than a humble baker. All I wish is for you and Gretel to be happy until the end of your days."

# Chapter Fourteen

GRETEL

THE DAY of Samhain was here. All the yearning that had consumed me for the past few months would be fulfilled, if all went well—but it would also be the day we left the bakery and the Magus became king again. As dusk fell, the Magus came downstairs in his costume. He was dressed in a black mask made with sharp, reptilian lines and small horns at the edges, like the face of a dragon, and he wore a cloak of fabric cut like wings that shimmered like dragon scales. His vest fit him closely and it was made of tiny leather scales.

"You look very menacing, Sir Dragon," I said. "And verrry handsome."

He tried not to look too pleased. "Take off your clothes, Gretel. All of them. Tonight, if all goes well, you will be mine."

I shivered with anticipation and a little bit of anxiety. "Do you have a costume for me?"

"Put on the dress you have embroidered so beautifully with the horses on the skirt," he said.

I hesitated. If he wanted me to put on the dress first, that meant no blouse.

"What's stopping you?" he said.

"I—I don't want anyone to see my breasts," I said. "Except you. I don't like other people to look at me the way you do."

"A request I am happy to oblige," he said. "No, that was never my plan. I never meant for anyone to see you. I like to have these sacred parts of you all to myself. But first things first."

By now I was so accustomed to constant stimulation and a feeling of fullness inside me that I felt empty, almost bereft, as I stripped off all my clothes. My pussy yearned to be touched and teased. But soon I would not have to wait any longer. I put on the dress and let him lace the bodice as he always did. I liked that I could feel his touch by the way the ribbons tugged around me, hugging my breasts and offering them up to him. I watched the serious set of his mouth as he tied the bow and I imagined him taking my nipples between his teeth.

I chewed my lip furiously.

"Here is your cloak, my Gretel, very modest as you can see." He gave me a short hooded cloak that fell to my elbows. It went over my head and did conceal my breasts... but how easy it would be for his hand to find them. The little hood had a fringe of fur in back a little like a horse's mane.

"You get to be a dragon and I'm just a horse?" I asked.

"No, you are a unicorn, my dear." He gave me a pearl-edged white mask with a horn made of crystal to sprout from my forehead. "A much more appropriate pairing."

White stockings and little heeled black shoes

completed the ensemble. Before we set out, we looked in the small mirror by the door and although I was not much for giggling, I may have let out some sort of embarrassing squeak of glee. He was all in black and adorably grumpy looking which I knew was covering up his nerves, while I was fair and more than a little bit aroused. By now, nothing needed to stimulate me for me to feel a thrill of anticipation.

I was nervous, too, when I considered what this night meant. If we failed, the Magus would die. If he succeeded, I would be his queen. My mind could not fully accept either of these things. Somehow I felt that we would come home to this cottage, and I clung to that thought. It was better to enjoy the moment than worry about what the night would bring.

We walked together down the path to the Revels, and at one point I almost forgot myself and grabbed his hand.

I could hear the music from quite a distance. It rumbled under our feet. It was soon clear to me that the Wicked Revels had more musicians than I had ever heard, and certainly of more skill. My ears felt like they belonged to a wealthy woman; we never heard music of such quality in a poor town like Aupenburg. Up ahead, our path crossed another and I saw other faeries dancing along. The musicians were on the move with them in a procession, and everyone was dressed in costumes.

"We are coming to the Three Precious Groves," he said. "This is the gateway to the Revels. Normally, the humans and the revelers are separated by barriers of magic. You can't travel freely between the worlds unless you know your way around magic—or unless magic decides to have its way around you. But on this night, the walls are so thin that anyone can travel between them."

I watched them dancing by, girls in hats and dresses

made of fluttering flower petals of silk, others wearing robes spangled with stars and the costumes of bygone queens. The men were knights and fearsome beasts in masks, with claws and fur. Others were tricksters and fools and beggars, and a few wore robes from foreign lands. One hunched figure wore a horned skeleton for a mask and carried a staff with a glass eye mounted on the top. Two dark knights rode black horses with red eyes. Their armor was black and red to match. I spotted a harpy that looked like an actual harpy and not a costume at all, although I had thought them extinct.

I shivered.

"Are you frightened, Gretel?" the Magus asked, with a hint of surprise.

"Where are they going?"

"To Pillna. They will knock at the doors of the humans and ask for food."

"I must admit...I'm not sure I would want to see them at my door."

"If the humans give the faeries food, they will have no trouble at all. If they refuse, well...just a bit of mischief. But that isn't what *we're* here for. I just want to keep an eye on things, and I'll speak to Will when the revelers return home."

"I see."

I suppose I had not fully considered that the Magus was a faery. I had always been warned against faeries, but he seemed human to me. This lot, I wasn't sure I trusted and I couldn't help but feel sympathies for the town of Pillna who had to deal with this strange invasion.

The king and queen were at the back of the procession, riding white horses. They wore cloaks of leaves and crowns of vines. We were still standing at a distance but even from here they had the serenity of royals who are in charge of a happy and prosperous kingdom. Tiny bells jingled on the saddles and bridles of their horses, over the pounding of the drums that had already passed by. They were followed by female attendants carrying their banners, dancing on light slipper-clad toes. I looked for Jeannie, but I didn't see her. She must be at home with her husband by the fire, watching the royal children.

The Magus was stiff as he watched them, and then he looked around the forest. Once the banners passed, there was a detail of guards and then the path was clear behind them. It started to feel quieter in the forest almost immediately.

The Magus tore his gaze away from the trees and moistened his lips. He waved his hand toward the path. "Come on."

"Is something wrong?"

"I don't see Aramy nor any of his kin."

"You did speak to him, didn't you?"

"I don't trust Aramy very much."

We walked slowly, so we wouldn't catch up to the King and Queen. The forest started to grow thinner above us as we got closer to town, and I could feel in my bones that we had stepped out of the faery world. The air took on a strong smell of woodsmoke very suddenly and I saw the glow of torches ahead. The town was well lit on this night, and the faeries brought still more light into it, and a great deal of noise. By the time we were walking past the houses on the outer edges, the faeries were running all through the streets. I heard pounding and singing and shouting and footsteps racing down dark alleys.

My pulse pounded. On this night, I couldn't help but feel human, and wish it would end. I knew the townsfolk must be nervous.

"I'm surprised King Will still lets this go on, if he's a human," I said.

"He would be a fool to stop the ritual. This is how we burn off the tension of centuries between faeries and humans without anyone getting killed. It's better to play tricks than go to war."

We walked down a street with shuttered windows. Ahead, two faery men in gargoyle masks pounded on a door. An old woman answered and dropped two paper-wrapped caramels into their waiting hands without a word. They ate them on the spot as she quickly shut the door. Then they ran to the next house.

"That poor old woman!" I said, indignant. "She was terrified of them! This isn't right. Maybe I do want you to be king just so you can find a way to—make this better."

"When it's over," the Magus said, "the humans who gave to the faeries will find that their gardens are abundant next year, and their cows give more milk. Not a bad trade for two caramels. You must think more like a faery now, my dear. It's a game we play. No need to feel real fear. You know how that is, don't you?"

"Well...I guess I do."

He smiled and pulled his wand out of his cloak, and my whole body shivered with anticipation of something being done to it, out of pure reflex. Instead, he turned to the old woman's door and knocked.

"Please don't bother her!" I cried.

The door creaked open and she looked up at his height, then held up a caramel with a faltering hand. He took it in the palm of his glove and tossed a coin into her hands in its place. "I apologize on behalf of my kin for keeping you awake and giving you a fright," he said. "A blessing on your house." He tapped his wand against her door.

"Oh... that's very kind of you," she said, with relief. "Have a good night, sir."

When the door shut, he shot a look at me. "Is that better, Gretel?"

"Well, *yes*." I felt more relief than I should. "Can we just get a drink at the inn while we wait? I'd like to see if Anna's all right."

"Of course she's all right." He started walking that way, humoring me.

We came to the town square. Fires were burning, and some of the faeries were dancing around them. King Will stood in the shadows on his horse, keeping watch. I spotted the inn from here, and I saw several wiry little faeries pounding on the front door. No one answered, although there were lights inside. The faeries jeered and pitched eggs at the windows.

The Magus glanced around again, clearly not wanting to attract Will's attention. "We'll wait for that crowd to leave, then skirt around the back to the alley beside the inn," he said.

We ran down the streets and slipped around the rear of the buildings, sticking close to the shadows. I tried the door and was surprised when it opened.

The interior was crowded with men, dozens of them— almost as many in number as the revelers. They held swords and axes and other menacing blades and tools, and they stood up when I walked in the door. I tried to step back and a man was waiting to shut the door behind us, cutting the Magus and me off from the faeries outside.

At the forefront of the crowd was Hansel, and he had Peter at his side.

"Gretel," Hansel said. "I'm sorry, but I'm taking you home."

# Chapter Fifteen

GRETEL

"I GOT YOUR LETTER." He grabbed my arm and I tried to pull away. The Magus flicked out his wand, but didn't make a move. A hundred eyes were on him.

"Then you would know I'm perfectly happy and I don't need you meddling in my life!"

"I just can't let you do this," he said. "I can't let you spend your life with a man like this. He's bewitched you. I knew I should never have left you behind. Let's start over. I have a better job working at the cloth markets. I was always good with sums, as you know, and it's a much better fit for me. I can support you. And Peter's working as a tailor's apprentice. We have an apartment right by the sea, with a spare room."

"Well, good for you," I said sharply. "Good for you both, going to do what you want, living happily ever after. But of course you still have to order *me* around."

"Listen to your brother," said a gruff older man in the

crowd, holding a machete. "The faeries are menacing our town and we've had enough of it. Stay safe with your brother. You don't want to be a faery bride."

"Who says I don't?" I was quite tired of being told what I ought to do.

The men started moving to the door, nodding to one another. A couple picked up shields or helmets or medical kits, battered relics from old wars.

"Wait! What are you doing? Don't hurt them!" I cried.

The human men were pouring out the door in a wave of glinting steel and glowing torches, bellowing war cries. I could do nothing to stop them but only moments after they ventured out in the night, I heard screams.

"Hansel, this isn't right." I was begging him and he didn't pay any attention. He was looking at the Magus with pure hatred.

"Gretel, just stay out of the way," he grunted. "It's between me and him."

"No, it's not. It's between me and *you*. This was my choice, Hans. I told you in the letter."

"So I'm just supposed to sit back while my sister dishonors herself?" His eyes raked me up and down, like he saw beneath my modest garb.

I flushed with shame. I was happy with the Magus, but seeing Hansel's disapproval, I couldn't help but see myself in the church at Aupenburg again, wrestling with my feelings, wondering why I seemed to feel differently from everyone else.

"I wish you would understand me," I said, but the words felt feeble. Who didn't wish to be understood? It was too late for that.

The Magus flicked his wand at Hansel and knocked him back, so he had to release my hand. Hansel pulled out a long knife that had belonged to my father, and lunged at the Magus. I grabbed a tin plate off one of the tables and smacked him with it. It was a very ineffective smack, I'm afraid. Hansel was still much stronger than me and the plate was flimsy.

"Hansel, please! Don't fight!"

Hansel swung the knife and almost got the Magus, but my love was as graceful as he appeared, and stepped back just in time. He struck Hansel with another spell, knocking him into the counter.

Hansel ignored my pleas and attempted to kick the Magus, a move which was easily dodged—but I didn't notice Peter had snuck behind the counter and crept up behind the Magus. He struck the Magus in the head with a club.

The Magus' long legs staggered. He caught himself from falling, gripping the edge of a table. Peter swung again, and I tried to scream as the club barely missed the Magus' skull this time. A blow to the head was serious. When I was a child, a man had died from a single kick to the head from his horse. I was so panicked that a strangled sound came out of me, instead of a proper scream.

The Magus drew himself up again. His face was in shadow, candles flickering behind him. All the energy in the room seemed to gather around him. "Hansel, I would rather you work things out with your sister without my interference, but clearly, you would rather deal with me. And so you should realize just what you are dealing with."

The Magus whipped his wand furiously and Peter's body flew backward, unconscious and crumpled. Hansel screamed and flew to his side.

"You fiend!" he spat at the Magus. "Peter?" Hansel clutched the sunburnt, freckled face. "He's alive...but he needs help."

"I am a mage. You are a boy," the Magus said. "Tell me,

Hansel, did you have a hand in all this? Encouraging the human men to fight my people with swords and clubs? Because you were angry at me for capturing the attention of your sister?"

Hansel's mouth opened and shut. He looked too scared to speak, but also somewhat defiant. I imagined the Magus saw a strong resemblance between us.

"I have never laid a hand on your sister, but tonight I will ask her to be my bride," the Magus said. "If she says yes, and you try to stand in her way, we will be enemies then. Come on, Gretel," he said gruffly, urging me to the door.

I really didn't know what to do. I let the Magus pull me away but once we were out the door I started sniffling. He shot a sideways glance at me as he led the way to an empty alley that seemed safe enough.

"I'm sorry," I said.

"Hansel is never going to accept your choices. You've explained it to him, you've written him letters, and he should be able to see that you're looking well, but none of that matters to him. For some people, it is simply easier to decide how things should be early on, and never change one's mind."

"So I should never see him again?"

"Would you like me to tell you a lie?" the Magus said. "That he will ever accept you as you are?"

I didn't know what to say, and it was just as well, because the town was chaos around us and I could hardly ignore it. Human men were grabbing faeries and beating them, while the faeries fought back with magic. Sparkles and glimmers of colored light lit up side roads and shot through the square. The town had erupted into shouting, screaming and sounds of destruction. King Will was galloping around the fountain, bellowing out something over the din, while Queen Evaline tried to get to safety. Human men with axes blocked her exit. I saw their blades flash as they lunged at her. Her horse wheeled around as she tried to flee the other way.

The Magus looked around. "Gretel, I need to get you to safety."

"Don't worry about me. I can hide somewhere." The scene was overwhelming my senses. It had all happened so fast.

*Hansel had something to do with this attack.* He hadn't denied it. I could imagine him riding into town with my letter clutched in one glove, asking after me. The townsfolk, already suspicious of faeries, were happy to listen to his complaints. *Maybe they have some reason to be suspicious of faeries, but Hansel is so blinded by wanting to rescue me that he was willing to stir up a mob.*

Now, what had been an evening of mischief was turning into a battle, and people might die on both sides.

"I want to talk to Hansel alone," I told the Magus. "Just once. Please. I love you, but I love Hansel too, and I have to believe you're wrong. People can change."

"I can't let anything happen to you. Aramy will be here any moment."

"Hansel won't hurt me. But this is bad for the poor faeries." I saw the king storming his horse into the midst of some human men grabbing a faery girl. He ordered them away from her, only for them to try to pull him off his horse. He was forced to strike one of them with the blunt edge of his blade and then trample past the others, off to intervene on behalf of two faery boys who were back to back holding tree branches as feeble weapons. "You used to be the king. Isn't there something you can do?"

# Chapter Sixteen

## THE MAGUS

GRETEL HAD a way of looking at me that seemed to reflect my own soul back. She saw the good in me, where many would not—but she also understood my flaws. My pride. She looked at the struggling king, and she looked at me, and then she flew back to the door of the inn.

I let her go, although I wanted to follow her.

When I was the king, I knew the magic of the Revels, the trees and forests. If Will had proper instruction, he would immediately grasp the situation. He could have put up a fog and all his people could have fled into it, back to the faery realm. The humans might have followed since it was Samhain night, but at least we would be on our own turf. They might not dare.

But no, Will was a human. A former soldier. He defaulted to the human ways of fighting. He had no one to show him the ways of faery magic. He didn't have the old

king to guide him, as I had. Marte was unlikely to be help-
ful. This was how I had kept Gretel undetected, after all,
even when she broke the rule of my sentence. Will could
hardly enforce his own rules. But he was right in the fray,
fighting for the faeries as fiercely as anyone.

"Curse it all," I muttered. "The things a woman can do
to a man." I strode toward Will and used my wand to
knock aside the men surrounding his horse.

Will saw me, and he edged back a little, still keeping
his sword ready to strike. "Magus? Is that you?"

So much for a costume disguising me. My height and
form must have been recognizable.

"You're not supposed to be here with the Revels," Will
said. "Did you organize this attack?"

"No, I'm trying to save you from it. And believe me, I'd
rather not, but these are still my people. They're dancers
and musicians, not warriors. We need to get them out of
here quickly."

"I would love to, but how?"

"Summon a deep fog."

"Summon a deep fog?" Will repeated. "And just how do
I manage that?"

"You're the king. You feel a connection to the forest.
The conditions are right. Reach down inside of that
feeling and draw it up. The land will create the mist for
you and send it out to rescue you. I would do it if I could."

"But we're not in the faery forest." Will looked at me
in his damned human way, like he didn't quite believe me.
We didn't have time for this. The air smelled faintly of
smoke as one of the houses had caught fire—probably in
an attempt to burn the faeries—and a man was shooting
arrows at the harpy girl as she tried to take flight.

"The magic follows you. Just try it," I snapped. "Or

would you like me to take the time to explain it from top to bottom?"

"Fine," he snapped back. Will, no doubt, didn't like the suggestion because it had come from me. I couldn't blame him. I would feel the same.

Will led his horse a few steps away from me and his eyes briefly shut. I used my wand to fend off a few humans who tried to get close to him, giving him room to concentrate. I hoped he could manage it, because I could deflect with the wand, but I didn't have much in the way of offensive magic or weapons. That had never been my role. As King of the Revels, I had guards to fight for me, and a baker certainly had no time to learn to fight either. I kept watching the front door of the inn, waiting for Gretel, but she was still with Hansel.

The magic obeyed its king, impostor though he was. The fog started to roll in, obscuring my view of the inn. A thick layer of mist seemed to seep into the town from every direction, and soon no one could see much of anything.

"Fall back!" Will called. He drew up beside me. "Thank you."

"I just wanted to save my people."

"Is that all? I do wonder why you're here."

I still hadn't seen any sign of Aramy. Maybe he had gathered forces back at the Revels.

I could hear Gretel saying, *Have you ever apologized?*

"Magus," Will said. "I know why you're here."

I deliberately ignored my nerves.

"You've found yourself a girl and you want to touch her," Will said. "Your sentence officially ends tomorrow. But I appreciate the aid. I will commute your sentence now."

At first, I hardly comprehended the words. *I can touch Gretel...? I didn't even have to apologize.*

"Take my hand," Will said.

I hesitated to touch the broad, slightly calloused hand offered to me. I didn't trust his generosity. He must suspect my plans.

"One good turn for another," Will said. "That's all. I still don't want to see you at the Revels, but I also don't want to be in your debt. And I do like those cakes..." The hand didn't waver.

I reached for the hand, and I touched his skin. It didn't burn me. For the first time in three years, I felt the warmth of another being—just as I heard horses thundering down the hills surrounding Pillna, and the cries of invaders. I recognized the solid pounding of a battle drum, and it was all familiar to me, the sounds of my homeland.

Aramy was finally here, with the force from Ellurine. I should have been relieved.

Now I saw a memory of Gretel's face, stirring from sleep. *This is where you belong. Here with me.*

Will reached for the reins and our truce was forgotten. "What is that?"

*Are you sure you're not just repeating your old mistake in a different way?*

*I have to believe you're wrong. People can change.*

The horses pounded through the mist, trampling anyone who didn't get out of the way. The human offense against the faeries now seemed like a joke with a real army charging in. The faeries were forced to fall back, scattering in all directions toward the forest. They would find their way back to the Revels, no matter which path they chose.

I extended a hand toward one of the trees in the town square and pulled myself up into the branches for a better vantage point. I saw Deniel's banners fluttering above the sea of pale fog. My nephew led the charge.

"Deniel!" I shouted. "Halt! It's your uncle! I want to talk."

As Deniel stepped out of the fog, I heard sounds of female protest. My nephew had Queen Evaline bound, gagged, and slung across his horse. "Don't worry, lamb," he said. "I have no intention of hurting you, but you're much too wriggly."

"Mmph!" Evaline was trying to speak.

"No time to talk, Uncle," Deniel said. I had not Deniel as more than a child except in painted miniature; he was born shortly before I left Ellurine. Now he was about the age I was when I left home, and my little sister's son could have been my own, with the softly curling dark hair, strong but refined nose and slightly amused mouth that were traits of my father's bloodline. "This is our chance, when Will is away from the Revels. Everything looks to be in a state of convenient chaos already!"

"Wait." I held up my wand. "We're making a mistake. My people—Will's people—they're happy with him."

By the time I spoke the truth aloud, it no longer felt like a revelation. It had been true for so long. I had fought the truth. I had tried not to change, myself. But I had.

"I saw the Revels under Will's rule. I saw him singing to them, his fine voice and their laughter—all of it. Gods, I don't want to admit it, but when I was the king, I made a mess of everything. The Revels are merry and peaceful, as they should be. Put the queen down."

I could hardly look at Evaline, but I saw her anyway, out of the corner of my eye. She stopped wriggling, and her eyes softened at me.

Aramy was behind Deniel. The old, retired baker and my handsome young nephew exchanged glances.

"You warned me, Aramy," Deniel said. "I'm sorry, Uncle, but you're talking madness. The Revels belong to our clan. If you don't want them, believe me—I do. Forward!" he shouted at his men. "Capture Will!"

The drums started back up in earnest and the horses charged around the tree where I was perched. I dropped back to the ground and ran for the inn.

# Chapter Seventeen

GRETEL

I REFUSED to believe that I had to give up my brother forever.

But the Magus had a point. For years now, I had been trying to convince my brother to allow me the same freedom he allowed himself. The argument always ended at the same impasse. He had already made up his mind that men and women had a different set of rules.

If I wanted him to understand, I had to make him see.

When I walked in, at first I didn't even see Hansel. The room appeared empty of people. Food had been upturned in the haste to leave.

"Hansel?"

"Over here..."

Hansel's voice came from behind the souvenir counter. Peter was unconscious.

"Is he all right?"

"I—I hope so. He hasn't woken up, but his breathing is

steady. I thought it would be safer for him back here," he said. He looked at me with a face more familiar to me than my own. I had looked upon that face for more days of my life than I could count. Across dinner tables and fires, my brother and I had laughed and cried together.

"How did we grow so far apart, while we were so close?" I asked. "Every day spent together, and I never knew you were in love with Peter."

He shrugged a shoulder.

"Gretel, I'm still not sure I understand...what *you* want," he said. "What is it you wanted all this time? Just... to...lose your virginity?" He dropped his eyes back toward Peter. "Look, brothers and sisters shouldn't talk about these things."

"No, Hansel...that's why I don't know how to tell you. But you're afraid for me because you don't understand, so I guess I have to tell you something. I have always been drawn to sensual experiences. To colors and music and rich foods, sure, but also...feelings. In the faery world, it isn't strange to acknowledge the pleasures of the body all the time, for sex to be a part of daily life. The Magus understands what makes me happy. I want to be with him. But— he has not been able to touch me, not once. Tonight, I pray...his curse will be lifted."

"He truly hasn't touched you?"

"No."

We were silent for a little while. I found some blankets in a closet to support Peter's head.

His brow furrowed. "You seem so different. I don't like it."

"I'm happy and not starving. I don't think I should have to tell you everything. You seem different too, you know."

"I don't know what you want me to say."

"I want you to knock it off!"

"He hurt Peter."

"And Peter hurt him." I was getting frustrated now. "I don't want to go in circles forever. I don't want to lose you either. I want to help you get Peter to a healer, and start over."

The door opened behind us and the Magus appeared. Shouting and thumping noises outside briefly grew loud until he shut the door again. His pale skin was sweating, but his expression remained calm. No matter how he looked, I was always happy to see him, a wave of anticipation sweeping across my whole body. Tonight, separated from him and denied any of the usual stimulation, I had realized how well all the drawn out teasing had trained me to feel pleasure even in my own mind.

But I had also learned to work through it, to decorate cakes and dip berries into chocolate in the most careful of gestures and keep my mind engaged, ignoring the scream of hunger inside me. It was a balancing act that had made me more aware of everything I was thinking and feeling.

"What's happening?" I asked.

"My nephew has brought a force from Ellurine. I thought Aramy was bringing my nephew to support my claim to the throne, but apparently, when I asked Aramy to swear he wouldn't kill Will, he started making plans to go around me. I was just about to make a tentative truce with Will when they appeared. Aramy and all the faeries who once supported me now want to put Deniel on the throne."

I had not expected this. "Then—what do we do?"

"They've captured Queen Evaline. They're trying to scatter the Revelers. I don't know what they plan, but we should assume the worst. It was already a mess before they arrived, and they're taking advantage of it. Mobs are not known for their good sense."

"Magus." I looked at him, praying he knew what he must do.

His head tilted like he had smelled something unpleasant. "I need to get back to the faery realm, call the horses, and fight...with Will. Time has almost run out for me. Come here, Gretel." He held out his hand.

I rushed to his side but of course I didn't touch him.

He grabbed my hand.

And held it.

An absolute thrill ran through me and for a moment all I could hear was the roar of all my unfulfilled desires pounding in my ears. I was touching him. I felt his skin, his hand engulfing my own in masculine warmth and strength. My eyes searched his face. *I don't understand. How?*

"Soon," he whispered to me. Then, to Hansel, "Hansel, you encouraged the humans to fight back tonight, didn't you?"

"They were already upset," Hansel finally said. "I just said I was looking for my sister."

"Well," the Magus continued, "if my nephew takes over the Revels, he's an impetuous young man. I don't think he will let this incident go without taking revenge on you, if you don't leave immediately. Whether or not you leave, he will take revenge on the people of Pillna. Will, on the other hand, is a human. He is far more likely to understand and forgive. If I were you, I would reconsider my allegiances."

"Peter needs a healer," I said. "Can Hansel come with us?"

Hansel hunched his shoulders in unconscious defense.

"Yes," the Magus said.

I saw faint relief in Hansel as he picked up Peter in his arms. I didn't let go of the Magus' hand for even a second while we hurried outside, with Hansel behind us.

The Magus stopped and waved some of the faeries onward, knocking back humans who pursued them. "Go, go," he said. "Get back to the Revels."

A few of them paused at the sound of his voice. "My lord...is that you?"

"I'm the baker," he said.

When he had aided as many faeries as were in the vicinity, we forged through the mist ourselves, hearing sounds of fighting we could no longer see, the Magus leading us toward a path leading back to the forest.

"How is it that we can we touch?" I finally asked.

"I helped Will fight off some humans, and he ended my sentence then and there. A mere few hours early."

"So, then—" I tugged on his arm, forcing him to stop hurrying, and I tugged on the tie of his cloak and tried to kiss him.

Instead, my unicorn horn collided with his dragon mask.

He laughed gently, pulled off his own mask, and pushed mine up to the top of my head. Our lips crashed together, sweeter than any confection I had ever tasted. I had been waiting for this forever and a day, and every faint touch of his skin to mine was like fire. My whole body thrummed with wanting. I hardly cared if Hansel saw us. I could hardly believe that I was permitted, now, to let my fingers explore the contours of his face as our lips and tongues joined with almost violent hunger. I nipped his lower lip just as he pushed me back.

He made a little growl of desire. "Soon," he said again. "It's not safe yet."

We kept moving, and we came to a grove of trees with

silver leaves. "We've made it. The gateway to the Revels," the Magus said. The mist was still thick here, too, but we had lost most of the humans. Faeries were fleeing through the trees; I saw ghostly, costumed heads float by over the fog, hair flowing as girls ran home.

We passed through groves with leaves of gold and translucent leaves that glinted like icy diamonds, and then we came to a gently flowing river. The dark trunks of trees stood in silhouette against its moonlit waters. Beautifully carved wooden boats were crossing, some of them swamped with faeries, others almost empty, but most of the boats were tied up on the other side of the bank. The harpy girl came soaring overhead.

"I'll swim across and get one of the boats for us," the Magus said. He quickly yanked off his boots, cloak and jacket, and ran into the water wearing just his trousers and a thin shirt. The water must have been fairly cold, but I could see bonfires burning on the opposite bank, so at least he could dry out there.

Hansel stood awkwardly, shifting Peter's weight in his arms. Peter started to stir.

"Peter?"

"Hans?"

Hansel lowered him to the riverbank. The other boy clutched his head. "How do you feel?" Hansel asked.

"Like shit, but I'll live." Peter laughed weakly. "I can't remember what happened. Are we safe?"

I was watching across the water. The Magus had almost reached the opposite bank, but men on horseback were riding up to meet him. They seemed to be waiting. He glanced back at me from a distance and then he reached the shore. They immediately tried to seize him and he knocked one of them off his horse and slipped past their grasp. I looked at Hansel, stricken. I'm not sure what

I was more afraid of: that he would be hurt by the other faeries, or that the Magus would be captured and we couldn't join before midnight. There were too many ways he might die.

"It's safer to stay here," Hansel said.

Just as I plunged into the cold water.

# Chapter Eighteen

·❦·

## THE MAGUS

I WITHDREW INTO THE WOODS, but I could see Gretel coming after me. The men didn't chase me because now they were watching her. I surveyed as much of the scene as I could from my vantage point, which wasn't ideal. I scrambled up a little higher on the bank. The mist was not so thick here. Deniel and the other men from Ellurine were charging into the Revels, and they were armed better than the costumed dancers could ever be. Ellurine had a proper army, while the Revels only had guards.

Deniel had ridden up toward the dais with the thrones. He already had Evaline, and he must be looking for Will now.

I looked at the moon. In the midst of all this, my own situation was becoming more dire. If I didn't join with Gretel, I would die, regardless of what other chaos was going on.

Some dark part of me couldn't help but wonder if

Aramy had been planning this long before our discussion the other day. It all seemed too convenient.

Gretel was almost at the shore, and one of the men dismounted and tried to go after her. She swam farther down the shore. "Magus!" she cried, and then she dove under the water.

I scrambled back down the bank, dead leaves under my bare feet. My sodden clothes were making me shiver but I hardly noticed. I emerged, shooting magic. The Ellurinans were starting to realize I only had one good offense, and getting knocked back wasn't that devastating if you knew it was coming. The man on the ground crouched, bracing himself for my attack. I ignored him and went for the horses instead. I didn't want to harm the horses if I could help it. I blasted their flanks, startling them, so they all went running with their riders forced to hang on.

Gretel popped up farther down the river. I changed course, running toward her instead. The man left behind on foot tore after me. I tried to knock him back, and he dodged my spell.

Gretel came toward me, at first wading slowly, and then running as more of her body came out of the water. She was still wearing her costume, unicorn horn, little shoes, and all, but it was soaking wet.

"Watch out!" she told me, and then she threw a few rocks at the man behind me. She must have picked them up off the riverbank when she went underwater. One of them hit his head and he stumbled and tripped on the brush.

"Ouccch," she hissed. "I hope I didn't kill him."

"I highly doubt that. But what else could we do? I'm glad you have good aim, my dear. This has turned into a huge mess, but Gretel...I'm almost out of time."

"Are you asking me if you can make love to me?"

"I'm asking you if I can fuck you quickly and make love to you later...which is not how I've envisioned it, but I still have to attempt to save Will's hide."

"Does this mean we can keep the bake shop?"

I took her hands. "Yes."

She smiled her magnificent smile. One could actually see it unfold from the center of her lips to the corners. "After all that, it just figures that I have to keep waiting for what I deserve. But...I couldn't be happier. All I've ever wanted is you, and our little home, and...miles of chocolate. Being king and queen could not *possibly* be better than all of that."

# Chapter Nineteen

✦

GRETEL

WE HURRIED UP A HILL, circling the Revels, as fast as we could run. Looking below us through the forest, I saw a vast clearing ahead, the size of a grand ballroom, or maybe much larger. It's not as if I had ever seen a grand ballroom. Fires burned around the perimeter, and I thought I saw some of our cakes on one of the tables, but no one was dancing or playing music. A faery sitting on horseback was addressing the revelers, who now huddled in their costumes.

"That's Deniel," the Magus said. "I'm not sure how this will be received..."

"The Revelers began thanks to the faeries," Deniel was saying, gesturing with his sword. "They need to stay in the family. Don't you agree?"

"I see Evaline, in the custody of one of his knights. Where is Will?" He tried to peer over the brush. "Damnit, I see him there on the dais. He's surrounded and he knows he's outnumbered, too. If only these woods still belonged to me."

"What can we do? If we find Will, can you tell him how to cast magic to stop this?"

He turned to me. "I should have helped him long ago, shown him how to harness the magic of the woods so he could protect his people in the case of invaders... It's too late for that."

"What about your own magic?" I asked.

"My magic enhances desire," he said. "That's about it. This wand only does parlor tricks."

"Yes, well...what does it enhance desire *for*?"

"You know what it does." He barked out a rough laugh. "The revelers' desire is enhanced by the magic. That's all. I don't know what you're getting at."

"How do you get the desire into the sweets? You take it from me, right?"

"Yes."

"Do you still have the caramel that old woman gave you?"

"I do..."

"And we must join quickly, right now. I'm about to feel you inside me for the first time. You've been giving me that damn potion so I can hardly orgasm if I tried. I can't help but wonder, if you took that magic and put it in the caramel, and gave that to Deniel... Maybe he wouldn't want to fight anymore."

He laughed. "That's ridiculous."

"Is it now?" I crossed my arms. "I can hardly think straight when you do the things you do to me. It's as good as a confusion spell or anything else that addles your head. I asked for it and he didn't, but all's fair in war...well, they say that, don't they?"

"Maybe you're right, but how am I supposed to get him

to eat it?" Then he put a hand on my shoulder. "Actually—it's not a bad idea..." He laced his fingers with mine. "First things first. And this is...a first. For both of us. However rushed and tense we may feel now, I want you to forget all that, if even for a moment. I'm not always the best at expressing or even admitting my feelings, but I hope you know..."

"I do," I said.

"I love you, my Gretel. For three years I've needed to find someone whom I could love, and the moment you showed up at my door..."

"I love you too."

"I wanted this to be special. I wanted it to be so that you would never forget a single moment of it."

"Do you think I will?" I shook my head. "I just don't want you to die, idiot."

"Oh, is that how it's going to be now?" He wrapped his arm around the front of my chest and pulled me against him. "Come with me, you saucy tongued thing. I know just the place to put you."

Now that he could touch me, the wand didn't need to tap me into place, and a wand could hardly compare to his confident fingers, the sensation of his chest pressing against my back. He took both my hands in one of his behind my back and urged me down a shadowed path, deeper into the forest. My heart immediately started skittering a faster beat, and it was already thumping along to begin with, thanks to all the tension of the night. We walked long enough that the noise of the faeries was distant, and came to a glade where the forest was not so thick. A soft blanket of moss covered the path, and moonlight illuminated the trees, which grew in strange twisting shapes.

They didn't grow like that naturally, I thought. They

were trained like the topiaries I had heard of in palace gardens. He led me to one of the trees which grew in a gentle downward slope, forking into two separate trunks that maintained the sloping shape until about nine feet from the base, where the tree finally started growing toward the sky. He kept pushing me toward the tree until I had to straddle the trunk, spreading my legs around it, my thighs hugging soft whitish bark.

He unfastened my cape and hung it on a smaller branch, baring my breasts. Then he took my hands and guided them up onto the two forks of the tree trunk. I felt two vines snake down and catch my wrists. Then he pushed my torso down into the fork between the two trunks. I was nervous at this new position, but I trusted him. I didn't fight his guidance. Anyway, I could feel his legs brushing the back of mine, and as I bent down, I realized I had to stand on my tip-toes—actually, I didn't have to stand at all. The tree would support me. The slope of the tree trunk pushed my ass higher, and I felt his hard cock press against me. I was all spread out, my arms spread out above my head like I was flying, my braid breaking free from how I had pinned it and falling past my head. My head was pitched slightly downward, but not so much that I was lightheaded. My breasts hung in empty air, and all I could see was the dewy ground.

I moaned.

"Comfortable?" he asked.

"How do I answer *that*?"

He stroked his hands up my thighs and flipped up my skirt, which was still somewhat wet from the river. If anything was making me uncomfortable, it was my sodden clothing, but the air was surprisingly warm here.

Or maybe I was just getting very, very hot.

His hands cupped my ass, kneading my buttocks, and I

felt him crouch. Suddenly, I felt his mouth open around the pearl of my desire, his soft breath and then his lips and tongue drawing it into a cave of pleasure. He sucked hard and I shrieked. I could barely even see, the sensation was so strong and unexpected. One would think I was used to stimulation by now, but it was true that everything before this moment had only been a tease. Nothing compared to *him*.

His tongue traced expert lines around the most sensitive places, and I was speechless. Only when he stopped for a moment did I gather my wits enough to gasp, "You must hurry."

"I've been waiting so long to do these things to you. And we have to get some powerful magic into the caramel. You must indulge me. I doubt it's been more than a minute, although it might feel like a lifetime to you."

"Please, just—just get it over with for now. Later, we can— Oh, god!"

His tongue was on me again, but now his hands had reached up to pinch my nipples at the same time. He had never done anything to my nipples before. It was completely uncharted territory of sensation. I was nothing short of a mess in no time at all, whimpering and quivering, my arms sagging against my bonds, my legs heavy against the tree trunk, while my inner muscles and abdomen clenched without relief. The moment I felt him stand up again, I lifted my ass to press against him, almost unconsciously.

"Are you eager, my dearest?"

"Yes—yes, Magus." I paused. "Now, will you tell me your real name?"

"Corentyn."

I don't know why, but it almost made me cry, just to have a name for him. A real name, a real person, a boy from Ellurine who became a king, a king who became a baker mage—and mine.

"It's all right if you don't care for it."

"Why wouldn't I care for it? It's yours. Or—" I grinned. "Is it too workaday?"

He chuckled. "No, not that, at least. I suppose I'm not used to it."

"Well, you'd better get used to it, because I might be screaming it out quite often."

"Are you ready for me, my Gretel?"

"I've been ready since the day we met."

I couldn't really see what he was doing, and so the exact moment would be a surprise. I heard his trousers loosen and then he leaned over me, lifting my braid away from my face again, pulling my head up slightly. He gently kissed my neck and then slowly slid his tongue from my earlobe up the curve of my ear. My braid fell again, and his hands found my nipples once more. Almost the same moment as his hands took hold of my breasts, I felt the head of his cock push into me. Although nothing so large had penetrated me before, I was well prepared for him. I felt sorry for every bride who had no experience of such things, because for me there was no pain or shock, only sheer exquisite pleasure that I finally had the real thing filling me up, stimulating my skin in what felt like a thousand different angles. It was just a relatively small part of me, but I seemed to feel him everywhere, my skin tingling along my back, my arms, my legs, down to my fingers and toes.

He went slow at first, finding a rhythm, and despite my position I had some room to move with him. I could not be passive now; I wanted to make him fuck me harder as much as I could. Just as we worked together, we didn't say a word now. He felt what I was doing. I could sense the moment he understood that I wanted to take all of him, as hard and deep as he could give.

And once he did—

My entire soul surrendered to the feeling. His cock drove into me, again and again, his shaft both soft and as hard as steel, dismantling me from the inside out.

Of course, I knew it would end tragically for me. Soon I felt his hot, pulsing juices filling me as he clutched my breasts more firmly. "Gretel...my Gretel. Now you're truly mine, and you're all I could ever want."

"Corentyn." I wept his name. "I know we have to stop, but..."

He slid his hands up my arms, freed me from my bonds, and turned me over into his arms in one easy motion. I was limp as a doll and he felt so strong.

He held up the single caramel, wrapped in paper. "This would break a king," he said. "And once we've gotten rid of that young upstart of a prince, I will make it all up to you a hundredfold. I was once the king of pleasures. And if you are always my queen, I will always be your king. All my attentions are for you now. Believe me, my dearest, your sweet little self will never want for anything again."

# Chapter Twenty

THE MAGUS

I'M NOT SURE a crueler task was ever asked of a man than to pull myself away from Gretel to save Will, but I did what I must. And I knew I had to hurry. Every moment I had lingered with Gretel was already a dangerous move.

Still, I knew the revelers preferred negotiation to fighting, and I hoped that would take time. When we straggled into the grove, the musicians were pleading their case to Deniel.

"Will might be a human born, but he's a faery now! Please, your grace—"

"Humans can't turn faery," Deniel scoffed. "Any more than faeries can turn human."

"But sometimes a person has the soul of someone else. Aren't you the heir of Ellurine? Why not stay there?"

"Who wants to be king of Ellurine? Someone telling me what to do all the time?"

"I understand," I said, announcing myself. "I was once

the Prince Corentyn, then the King of the Revels. I became the latter to escape the former."

"Mmhm," Deniel said impatiently. "I've heard the story. Everyone has."

"You've heard the beginning. Maybe not the end. What do you desire from this place? Dancing? Parties? Good food? Pretty girls? Ellurine has all of those things."

"Freedom!" Deniel said. To him, it was obvious, as it had been to me.

"I thought the same thing," I said. "But in fact, no king is free. Kings have a great responsibility. The Revels might look like an escape, but in fact, they must be treated with care. Will understands this in a way that I never did, I hate to say. If I really wanted to be a king, I should have stayed in Ellurine. I assumed Ellurine would never change for me, when I should have changed Ellurine instead."

"It sounds like a damnable lot of work to change that place—you know how it is."

"I certainly do. And you're right. But who will be king of Ellurine if you stay here?"

"My little brother."

"Is that the life you want for him?"

"Well, no—"

"Wait a minute," Aramy said, interrupting just as I thought I might not even need the caramel. "My lord, I saved your life. I dealt with the Trickster Mage—"

"You made a bargain you said was meaningless anyway," I reminded him.

"Well, I should have known better! I've just gotten a letter from Vermon from a girl who says she's my daughter with that pretty little dancer who was here some fourteen years ago. You should see this letter, my lord—lovely penmanship, beautiful writing, she spins the finest thread, and she sent me a miniature of her face. The girl is the spitting image of my own dear departed sister. Now she wants to come here and what am I supposed to tell her? The Trickster Mage will come for her instead?"

"That *is* why he's called the Trickster Mage," I snapped. "Aramy..." I kneaded my forehead, which had sprouted a few lines of chagrin since I'd been brought back to life. "I appreciate that you brought me back to life. I truly do. I know it was the only way. But if you are truly loyal to me, listen to me now. You've given me your bake shop, and I have never been happier. Retire in peace and know that you served your king well."

"You are no king of mine anymore." Aramy drew his sword. I knew he wasn't very skilled with a sword, but I still didn't want to fight him. "Don't listen to him, Prince Deniel. All of this should be yours. It belongs to your family, not a human cripple."

Will drew his sword as well, and that prompted all of Deniel's soldiers and the clans who supported him to draw weapons.

"I might have a stiff leg, but don't underestimate me," Will said. "I've survived a war. I earned the Revels. If you want me gone, you'll have to fight me first."

"Will!" Evaline cried. At least Deniel had untied her. "Please, don't be proud and stupid!"

Will and I were actually rather alike, in many ways, I realized.

Few of the revelers had weapons, so this could escalate quickly and my people would have little choice but to surrender. But Aramy would still need Deniel to play along.

Time for the caramel—if I could get him to eat it.

I took out the small wrapped sweet and looked at Will, but I stayed close to Deniel. "Will—this candy is infused with all the powers I possess. Take it and you'll win the fight! Catch." I threw the caramel a bit off on purpose, and I knew Will wasn't fast to dive for a fallen object. It was still a gamble, but this had to be somewhat convincing or Deniel would immediately suspect it. One of his men snatched it instead.

"Bring that to me," Deniel said.

I had to mask my relief. "Deniel, you don't want to do this."

The young man rushed it to Deniel, eager to serve. Deniel unwrapped the caramel. "You want to spend your days making confections, Uncle? Let's see if they're any good."

He popped it in his mouth and chewed. It stuck to his teeth as caramels tend to do. His expression shifted quickly from defiant to curious and then took on a warm glow. "Moon and stars..."

"Are you all right, my lord?" Aramy asked nervously. He shot a look at me.

I gave him a brief smug grin.

"Yes," Deniel said. "This is—holy hell. The flavor—"

"I think you might have been enchanted," Aramy said. "Spit it out."

"No way. If I've been enchanted, give me more of it. It's like the best fuck of my life but somehow it's just...a caramel. All this fighting just seems *stupid*."

"It's not stupid." Aramy clenched his fists. "It's your right as a faery."

"This is the whole spirit of the Revels infused in one bite, isn't it? You made this, Uncle?"

"It's my magic, yes. And Gretel's. It's the magic of desire, that's all."

"I've tried aphrodisiacs and love potions," Deniel said. "This is different. It's—joyous."

I looked at my darling Gretel. Yes, I could never have

made such magic without her. Everything I did to her was not just stoking desire, but also fulfilling desire. The magic came from a place she had asked to go. "Deniel, stay for a few days and I'll make you boxes of caramels. Take them back to Ellurine. See what happens."

Deniel sheathed his sword and shrugged at Will. "Sorry about all this mess, tying up your wife and such."

"It runs in the family," Will said, with what I found to be unwarranted sarcasm.

Well, we were never going to like each other.

# Chapter Twenty-One

GRETEL

EVEN IN THE midst of all this, I didn't forget Hansel. I was relieved when I spotted him among the crowd, with Peter beside him, although they looked a little lost. When the revelers erupted into cheers of relief and Will invited the soldiers from Ellurine to have first crack at the banquet tables, I went to my brother even before I went to my Corentyn.

"Gretel," he said. "I—I see there's no use stopping you from joining this world and leaving mine. I suppose that's what hurts, in the end. It's not what Mother and Father would have wanted for you."

I'm not sure Mother and Father would have wanted Peter for Hansel, either, but I decided not to say so. "I am not really leaving my home," I said. "It's going to be a part of me forever. The house, the farm, and you. There's nothing to say we can't write and visit. I'm not moving to the *moon*. But if what really bothers you is that I've changed, well, it's too late for that. You could lock me in the attic for the rest of my life but you could never change me back."

"Heaven forbid, I don't want to lock you in an attic," he said. "I know you're right. I'm not comfortable with this, but I don't want to lose you."

"You don't have to be comfortable, I suppose. Just tolerant."

Peter nudged him. "I suppose if we'd just accepted the situation, I wouldn't have gotten knocked out. This is pretty funny, when you think about it. It's like that time Marcus caught us kissing in the woods behind the school and I beat the daylights out of him."

"Please...Corentyn—the Magus—is going to ask Will to marry us," I told Hansel. "Will you stay for it?"

And so he did, and when the moment came, he didn't even look begrudging. It was a simple ceremony under the trees, and Will himself spoke the words to pronounce us husband and wife. He didn't really look begrudging either.

"Corentyn of Ellurine, Mage-Baker of the Revels, you and your wife are welcome back to the festivities—as long as you have time to keep making those cakes," he said.

Queen Evaline welcomed me herself after the ceremony, and Jeannie kissed my cheeks. "Good for you, dear. I like happy endings. Although I don't envy you yours. Didn't your husband just promise his kin a whole bunch of magic caramels?"

That was very true. I had a feeling I would never truly see the end of my torments!

But for now, we came home to a quiet house, and he scooped me into his arms and carried me over the threshold and up the stairs.

"Now," he said, "For once, I am going to make love to

you in a proper bed, and give you all the happiness you deserve."

"That *almost* sounds boring." I sat down on the bed and gave him my best mysterious smile. "

"Are you bored when I hold you in my arms?" He sat down beside me and pulled me into his lap. "That would be a shame."

"N-no, not at *all*," I said, melting into his touch. He took my braids down from their pins and loosened my plaits until my hair fell across my shoulders, with all the careful consideration he gave to everything. He looked at me with feelings I could not put into words. I had waited for him for so long, and I suppose he had waited for me even longer. He had gone three years without a single touch from another person. Now, his hands traced along my neck without pain. He loosened the ribbons of my bodice and brushed the fabric off my shoulders. I was properly clad in a blouse and undergarments now.

But not for long. He pulled my blouse over my head and then flung off his own shirt, and then held me against his skin. His fingers traced my shoulder blades and spine like he could never get enough of touching me, as if he had to feel every inch of me.

Holding me, he draped me down onto the bed and sucked my breasts, finally stirring my ravenous senses in the way I dreamed of. His teeth and tongue left no inch untouched, many times over, until the sensitivity of it was such that it had spread through my whole body. He tugged my skirt down and flung it on the floor, and when I was bared for him, he slipped two fingers inside me and started slowly pumping them as he stroked my bud.

"I've taught you how to wait, now I need to teach you the opposite," he said. "I have brought you to desire so many times, but I have never given you what you need.

Today, I am going to break you open. Are you ready for that?"

"Y—yes," I said, although the intensity of his expression might have given anyone pause—but heavens, I was wet. When his fingers worked in and out of me it sounded like he was stuffing a pastry with cream.

He took something out of his pocket—three little wooden shapes that reminded me of clothes pins. But they also reminded me of the slivers of wood that clamped around my clit. He put two of them around my stiff nipples and pinched them, manipulating the wood until he was satisfied. I arched my back, turning my head to the side so my hair draped across my face, trying not to writhe, all my sensations drawn closer and closer to the edge. Then, as I knew he would, he clamped the other one around my clit, tighter than it had been before. He wasn't just trying to tease me anymore. This was real. This was meant to make me come. Now I was incredibly sensitive and swollen there. A sheen of sweat broke out on my chest and forehead.

"Wait there, my sweet," he said. "Keep your little legs spread and don't touch anything."

I did want to close my legs, because that would let me use my muscles to move the clamp. I moaned, clutching at the blankets, as he took off his trousers. The sight of his naked muscles and erect cock gave me a surge of desire that seemed, at this point, almost unbearable, and yet more delicious than anything.

*I was about to eat the feast.*

He sat on the very edge of the bed. "Come and sit here," he said.

I pushed myself off the bed and walked toward him, quivering a little.

"Sit," he said again, putting his hands on my hips. He

hooked his feet around my ankles and spread me until there was nothing I could do but to sit on his cock. The anticipation, the tingling of all my nerves, as my sheath slid down his thick shaft—for a moment I thought I would break right then and there.

He picked me up like I weighed nothing and I wrapped my arms around his neck. He started kissing me and claiming me at once, holding up my legs, working in and out of me. Each thrust pressed against my clit and made it thrum in time with his cock on the inside, and I hardly even knew what he was doing anymore. I just knew that I felt something absolutely everywhere—his tongue pushing into my mouth, his hands stirring my skin and moving my body where he wanted it to go, the tight sensation on my nipples, his strong thighs under my legs, his pelvis thrusting deep.

I was overcome. The orgasm seemed to hit me not just between the legs but all over my body at once. I was flying in his arms—no, I was breaking apart, just as he said—no, I was turning into an ocean, a churning uncontrollable force of push and pull, my pussy clamping around his cock in pulsing waves of pleasure. I was screaming. I might have bit his lip again and I definitely yanked on his hair.

I could do nothing but let it ride through me, so intense that it scared me. I'm sure I knew why staid men of my old world didn't want women to feel this way. I felt like I was transforming into some supernatural being. Surely I must be able to shoot fire out of my fingers by the time this was over.

Finally, I bucked against the final pulses, cringing now against the pressure on my nipples and clit. "Coren, it's too much, it's too much."

"Shh, shh." He stroked my hair and my body slowly

started to relax around him. His cock was still stiff inside me.

We looked at each other, saying nothing for long moments, but my sobs turned to laughter. I was so relieved. And so was he. His eyes told the story. I touched his cheek and ran my hands through his hair, so happy that I could touch him whenever I liked, and just as happy that I would never have to share him with a kingdom.

"My king," I said. "Mine alone."

"My workaday girl, with plenty of work to do." He smiled. "Is it still too much?"

"No."

"Good," he said. "I'm not done with you."

"I hope you never are."

"I was the King of the Revels, my dear. I'm sure you would tire of me before I ever tired of you," he said.

But there was no need to worry of that.


THANK YOU FOR READING! If you enjoyed this book and you want to be extra-awesome, leave a review on Amazon. (They will ask you to give a star rating when you finish, but that's not the review...which is confusing.) And to make sure you don't miss a release, sign up for my mailing list, and come chat with me on Facebook! Is there a fairy tale you'd like to see? Drop me a line on Facebook or at lidiyafoxglove@lidiyafoxglove.com! A yuletide Little Red Riding Hood is next, but I'm also thinking about all the fairy tales I have yet to tell for 2018...

# Fairy Tale Heat Series

Every book is standalone and can be read in any order, although some characters might pop up in later books!

## About the Author

Lidiya Foxglove has always loved a good fairy tale, whether it's sweet or steamy, and she likes to throw in a little of both. Sometimes she thinks she ought to do something other than reading and writing, but that would require doing more laundry. So...never mind.

lidiyafoxglove@lidiyafoxglove.com

Made in the USA
Coppell, TX
10 January 2022

71345142R00094